QUARTET ENCOUNTERS

THE ROYAL HUNT

The Royal Hunt is distinguished by its penetrating exploration of the psychology of mass terror, and by its mythic projection of terror's dehumanizing effects on both individuals and entire communities. In a kaleidoscopic reconstruction of a physician's memories of the traumatic experiences of his childhood, the protagonist as a young boy discovers the wonders of sex, love and friendship against a sinister background of crime and terror that threatens to engulf the entire community of which he is a part.

For reasons that remain obscure, Kalagherovich, a country-level official of the Communist Party, is targeted for extermination and is therefore accused, in the classic manner, of being the 'agent of a foreign power'. He disappears mysteriously, and strange happenings occur in the lives of those involved in the plot, who manipulate events behind the scenes by exploiting what seems to be the sudden outbreak in the community of an epidemic of rabies. Inhuman violence erupts. Instinctive drives take over. Monstrous forms of desire are indulged. And a panic that may or may not be the true (and only) epidemic disease, and that is somehow contracted in morbid fear of its contagion, comes to grip the entire community.

D.R. POPESCU

Dumitru Radu Popescu was born in Romania in 1935. After studying medicine and the humanities he graduated with a degree in philology in 1961. A prominent journalist, he has edited the literary weekly *Tribuna* since 1970. He is a member of the Central Committee of the Communist Party of Romania and a member of the National Assembly. He was elected President of the Romanian Writers Union in 1981. He has written several collections of short stories as well as novels and plays. *The Royal Hunt*, perhaps his most celebrated novel, is the first of his works to appear in English.

D.R. POPESCU

The Royal Hunt

Translated from the Romanian and
with an Introduction by
J.E. COTTRELL and M. BOGDAN

QUARTET ENCOUNTERS

Quartet Books   London   New York

First published in Great Britain by Quartet Books Limited 1987
A member of the Namara Group
27/29 Goodge Street, London W1P 1FD

British Library Cataloguing in Publication Data

Popescu, Dumitru Radu
   The royal hunt.—(Quartet encounters).
   I. Title   II. Vînătoarea regală. *English*
   859'.3'34[F]   PC840.26.055

ISBN 0-7043-0044-3

Reproduced, printed and bound in Great Britain
by The Camelot Press plc, Southampton

Introduction

Dumitru Radu Popescu is probably Romania's best known contemporary writer. His works have been published in translation in many countries, including France, Germany, Italy, Sweden, India, Japan, and of course the East European countries. This translation of *The Royal Hunt* is, however, the first of his works to be made available to readers of English.

Author of more than twenty-eight volumes of novels, short stories, essays, poetry and dramatic works, Popescu enjoys great popularity and prestige in his own country; but he is also regarded as something of a paradox. At present he holds an official position as president of the "Writer's Union," and is also an appointed member of the Central Committee of the Romanian Communist Party; and yet, what makes Popescu a particularly fascinating writer is the vigorous attitude of political challenge and social protest so powerfully expressed in his novels and plays. Richly complex and insightful, but at the same time simple in their basic message, his works are difficult but accessible, obscure but profoundly illuminating. There have been more than fifty productions of his plays before large audiences in Romania and a number of productions abroad. However, one wonders how many of his numerous spectators take seriously the grave questions he raises in his entertaining theatrical pieces.

Born in 1935 in Păuşa, Bihor (Transylvania), to parents who were teachers, Popescu spent part of his childhood in a small village in Oltenia, in southwestern Romania, the setting of *The Royal Hunt*. Later, as a student at the University of Cluj he studied first medicine and then literature. He gained prominence as a literary figure during the "cultural boom" of 1968–71, when Romanian writers, in an unprecedented show of purpose and vehemence, brought their society to trial, focusing especially on the evils that afflicted it during the first decade of the "transition to socialism" (roughly 1950–60), a period that was so bitterly exposed and denounced in their writings that it became generally known in Romanian history as "the haunting decade" (*obsedantul deceniu*).

Popescu produced his best novels while working as a proofreader for the cultural journal *Steaua*. They belong to a massive cycle entitled *F*, which consists of seven volumes of novels published between 1969 and 1976, among which is *Vînătoarea regală*. Each volume (which is presented as a type of extended novel) is made up of several independent novels and novellas that are loosely related to each other and to the others in the cycle, but which may also be considered autonomous entities. Together they make up a frightening literary dossier of crimes and moral and political abuses. All are set in the world of a mythical county reminiscent of William Faulkner's fictional Yoknapatawpha County. It is the coherence of the fictional framework and the recurrence of the characters that give unity to these novels, as well as to the entire cycle.

The central character of the *F* narratives is a young prosecutor, Tica Dunarintzu, who pursues his own private investigations into the events that occurred in a Danubian county during "the haunting decade" and who seems to be the main driving force behind the relentless, virulent probe into the past that, in fact, leads to a verdict of guilt for many of the characters. The revelations that come out of this pathetic search for truth are often so tragic and terrifying that they give to the best of Popescu's novels their distinct appeal as documents of the mysterious paths of human motivation. In the words of leading Romanian literary critic Nicolae Manolescu, Popescu in these works is "the creator of one of the strangest, most original and most violent epic visions in all of Romanian literature."[1]

Vînătoarea regală (*The Royal Hunt*), published in 1973, in a volume of the same title with six other interrelated narratives, is one of Popescu's most representative writings and may be considered one of the most successful artistic portrayals of mass terror in contemporary literature. This vision of terror has often been compared to a similar image in *Rhinoceros*, by Eugene Ionesco (also of Romanian origin), a play that has come to be accepted as a "classic" of absurdist drama. Both authors present us with a world that is grotesque and at the same time terrifying, in which humans descend into bestiality. But while Ionesco's vision of rhinoceritis as a disease of conformity is presented in light of its comic aspects and is made to appear ridiculous in its repulsiveness, Popescu's view of a world that has been invaded by terror, disguised under the mask of cosmic rabies, impresses us as being more tragic and his style more poetic. Writing of the image that *The Royal Hunt* gives us of the "new" type of human emerging in the "new society," Manolescu perceptively notes: "Everything is mixed together, men and dogs, in a macabre vision of the birth of a new and horrifying species" (p. 165). The strength of this penetrating vision is further increased by the fact that it comes to us through the eyes of a young boy in a manner so natural the reader feels that the strange events recounted have a ring of authenticity and give the impression of being deeply rooted in a personal, emotional experience, as if one were listening in on memories from the author's own childhood in a village like Braniste.

Popescu's style may be compared to that of Gabriel García Márquez in *One Hundred Years of Solitude*, although it is more concrete and somewhat sharper, with the "mythic" elements being less immediately evident.[2] Furthermore, in Popescu's books the social and political critique has always had great impact on readers, and the mystery and suspense we find in his novels make them read somewhat like detective stories. It is, nevertheless, the mythical dimension that gives to Popescu's works their greater meaning, as it does to Márquez's. But where Márquez uses obviously fantastic elements as the main building blocks of his literary constructions, Popescu creates his world from elements that, although extraordinary, have the appearance of being realistic; only upon reflection does the reader notice that the narrative accumulation of these elements actually points to another realm of meanings, that they are in fact progressively animated and transfigured by a terrifying vision that gives them their supernatural dimension.

The overall narration of *The Royal Hunt* weaves a complex tapestry depicting the life of a small community in a relatively short but troubled period of time and the immediate, devastating effects of radical social change on the lives of even the common peasants in that remote village hidden in one of the far corners of the land. It is, however, much more than that. It is also a sensitive study of a young adolescent boy's coming of age in a world where fear and uncertainty continually lurk beneath the surface of everyday life; of a boy who discovered a terrible truth about himself and his fellow villagers: that they were all "on a road with no future, forced to live in a time and in a life with no future." In fact, *The Royal Hunt*, like Popescu's other works, may be read on several levels: on one narrative level it is the story or log of the traumatic experiences of a boy who witnesses strange, dramatic occurrences in the life of his village; on a second level it is a caustic judgment on social and political realities; but at its deepest level of meaning this novel is a penetrating exploration in the psychology of terror and a mythic projection of its dehumanizing effects on individuals and entire communities.

The boy, Nicanor, is actually an adult in the present tense time sequence of the novel, a medical doctor who recounts his childhood memories, prompted by his friend,

Tica Dunarintzu, who is trying to discover the facts surrounding his father's (Horia Dunarintzu's) death. Nicanor
is the only person still alive who witnessed what went on
in the village of Braniste during the time of the outbreak
of "rabies." He was the "crazy boy" who insisted on
walking around on stilts in order to be able to see everything from above and who hid to watch and listen wherever anything was happening or whenever people were
talking, displaying a typical adolescent thirst to learn
more about life, especially about love and sex. The novel
is a kind of kaleidoscopic construction of Nicanor's memories, related as if they were occurring then and there
before the eyes of the child who witnessed them long
before. Indeed, the child Nicanor, who is there still within the adult medical doctor, actually relives his past before our eyes.

A boy narrator as purveyor of information about such a
complex period of human history might seem to be an
odd artistic device, but it proves to be one that is perfectly
suited to the author's intent in this novel. Impressed by
what he observes, possessing the sharp perception of a
child who sees with wonder for the first time what has
become commonplace or predictable to adults, Nicanor
shows us the clear outlines of what occurred and was
recorded, infallibly, in his mind. His plane of vision (and
thus that of the reader) may be thought of as binocular, as
he looks at the events he remembers from the perspective
both of the participant-child and of the analytical adult.
The child's perspective is, however, by far the dominant
one as Nicanor focuses now on one part of the larger
scene, now on another, enlarging each to proportions
greater than life as he points out details one would otherwise overlook, details that are for us significant indicators
of the larger truths he senses but cannot articulate. At
first he understands little or nothing of what is going on
and only later does he see some meaning in what he has
witnessed and heard. He is a kind of Everyman who
would not have been aware of what was happening to

him, who would have been confused about the motives of those around him as panic spread through his world, and only later would have had an idea of what had occurred. The boy-adult narrator thus functions as an image of the consciousness of a society that is moving in a direction dimly perceived by its members, but whose destination is not yet comprehensible to them.

From Nicanor's recollections, presented to us in the psychologically authentic form of clusters of kaleidoscopic memories associated with specific painful or horrifying events, we can piece together some of the story about the central character of the main plot, Kalagherovich, a county-level leader of the Communist Party who (for reasons that remain obscure) was targeted to be destroyed—a local power struggle or a high-level ideological decision? The procedures used to get at him were the classic ones: he was accused of being the "agent of a foreign power" who had been infiltrated into the Communist Party, paid in dollars through the consul of that "foreign power" to engage in "criminal activities," one who was finally "proved" to be a "deadly enemy of the new society." But the genuinely original aspect of this familiar strategy was the killing of all the false witnesses that had been set up and the murder of those people who were at all sympathetic toward Kalagherovich, even before the assassins set about killing him. The even more extraordinary aspect of their plot was that the killers took advantage of an epidemic of rabies that *seemed* to strike the entire village at that time, bringing about mass panic in which all living creatures in the village suffered indiscriminately. The disease is interpreted by the unknowing peasants as a direct effect of breaking a ritualistic interdiction against hunting on a particular day of the year. According to the village legend, each year when people go hunting on that day, deliberately breaking the law, someone dies.

The novel begins in fact at that point: the people guilty of hunting are trying to ward off the possibility of a real death by faking the death of Big Prince in a family masquerade. From up on his stilts, Nicanor accidentally witnesses the "death" and "resurrection" of Big Prince and is consequently striken with a long illness in which he has nightmarish visions of the monstrous proliferation of death in his village, visions that prove to be prophetic. In his dreams he sees a red blanket that threatens to cover everything and to suffocate him; then his neighbors begin to turn into monsters, creatures that are half dog, half people, who eat humans alive. Just as he begins to recover from his illness, rabies seems to invade his village and strikes first the animals and then the people, who try everything they can think of in order to avoid contamination, including magic tricks like changing their names so that the disease won't be able to find them. But nothing can stop it; more and more people and animals die or begin to show bizarre symptoms of unnatural maladies, inhuman violence, instinctive drives, monstrous forms of desire, extreme fear, and hypersensitivity. It is not, however, the supposed disease itself that is the major problem, rather it is the villagers' terror of it and the panic it causes as people try anything to escape from its mysterious, fatal clutches. Nevertheless, the disease remains ambiguous to the reader. One cannot be sure if there really is an epidemic of rabies in Braniste, or if it is just a grotesque projection onto nature of the fears and paranoia that people are experiencing on the social level of their lives. As a study in mass panic, *The Royal Hunt* is certainly one of the finest in all of contemporary literature.

By the end of the novel, the three main levels (memorialistic, political, and mythic) are so deeply intermingled that they all fuse in the integrative image of a cosmic disease that encompasses the entire world of the text. At the instigation of the nurse (a good example of a "new society" type of person), all the men of the village go out with their dogs in a desperate attempt to escape from terror by "cleaning out" the "rabic forest" surrounding the village. In the end they sacrifice the only man who refuses to accept the rabies subterfuge, and who tries to uncover the truth about Kalagherovich. These are the same characters who participated in the masquerade of death at the beginning of the book; but now hiding a different nature under different names, changed from the hunted into ruthless hunters in need of a scapegoat. And this time their participation cannot be paid for with a fake death; they must commit a real crime, in painful counterpoint to the opening grotesque scene. The last image of the red sun sinking while the moon rises may suggest some hope in an otherwise grim ending.

Like many other prose works from Eastern Europe, *The Royal Hunt* is an allegorical construction whose major metaphors include the hunt, rabies, the dogs and their masters, the stilts, and the village itself, a typical Romanian village that looks like a long chain of houses strung out loosely along a road, hillside, or mountainside, but which is also a strongly-knit cultural entity. Often in the text there are allusions to historical realities known only too well to Popescu's generation, like the census-taking activity engaged in by school officials, or the system of redistribution of wealth and material possessions, whose effects on a village like Braniste were that most of the peasants ended up "as poor as their curs," and there was no corn left in the barn even for the Prince's rats. Stylistic devices themselves may impart thinly cloaked meanings of their own, like the typical political rhetoric in the verbal war of chapters 7 and 9, which reflects the kind of power struggles that go on within the Party, and the ways in which ideas and individuals may clash while claiming each to be representing the real Party line.

Typically Romanian is the attitude of mockery we find in this allegorical style, which in Popescu's novel produces an element of grotesque. The social forces that are the source of suffering and tragedy are, at the same time, made to appear absurd and ridiculous in such instances as the parody of the famous Leninist slogan about "electrification," or of those individuals who try to fall in line

with the new powers they can't even clearly identify and
look foolish and self-contradictory every time they open
their mouth or take a step. And it is precisely through the
innocent child narrator that Popescu is able to show, so
explicitly, what the child in the well-known fairy tale
saw—that the emperor has no clothes on.

Translating this novel has been more like dealing with
poetry than with prose. Furthermore, given the particular
difficulties of translating Romanian into English, a joint
effort of two translators seemed to offer the best chance of
success. In addition to trying to render its meaning
faithfully in English, we have also tried to retain the fla-
vor of the original text in its stylistic and allegorical
richness. Thus the sentences are long and complex in
English just as they are in Romanian, and whenever possible, word order (which is much freer in an inflected language like Romanian) has been retained because in
Popescu's poetic use of language it is often an important
device by which the reader is led to perceive what is occurring. For example, a movement may be mentioned and
then the object that is moving, or a sound may be de-
scribed and then the cause of it identified. We have also
attempted to match words carefully so that an unusual
word in its context in Romanian has been rendered by an
unusual word in English, and a common, old-rooted Romanian word has been translated whenever feasible by a
well-rooted English word rather than by a Latin-based
neologism. After much debate we decided to make one
important change in the appearance of the text. In our
translation direct dialogue has been separated from the
rest of the text, making it easier to read. It was, however,
with reluctance that we agreed to make this change because it seemed to us that the dialogue run on in un-
broken paragraphs did perform the function of indicating
a stream of consciousness flow of the narration. We hope
that the long paragraphs remaining in the translated text
(those that did not contain direct dialogue) will still serve
to reinforce the memorialistic aspect of the narration.

The names Popescu gives his characters are often meaningful or descriptive (like epithets) and always colorful. Unlike Popescu's French translators, for example, we decided it was imperative to try to find equivalents for these names in English. Place names and other proper names have, however, been left in Romanian, sometimes in slightly Anglicized spelling to be more suggestive of their pronunciation. There are also a very few cases when common words were preserved in their Romanian form (e.g., *tzuica*, a plum brandy that is a kind of national drink in Romania; *hora*, a well-known folkloric dance).

Whatever inevitable losses have occurred in translation, *The Royal Hunt* is, we feel, so skillfully constructed, so moving and meaningful that English-speaking readers cannot fail to be impressed by this unusually powerful narrative.

1. Nicolae Manolescu, *Arca lui Noe. Eseu despre romanul românesc 3* (Bucureşti, Minerva, 1983), pp. 140–65.

2. Rodica Boţoman, "Between Myth and Reality: The Novels of D. R. Popescu," *Dialogue* (1982), 9, pp. 9–24.

THE ROYAL HUNT

1

—What glory remains on earth unchanged, what creature with breath, what high majesty? And what worldly joy does not fall into sorrow? All are as vain as shadows, as alluring and fleeting as dreams . . . Only a moment, a brief moment, and all are consumed by death . . .

Through the window, from outside; on the table placed in the middle of the room was Big Prince with his hands crossed on his chest and a candle between his fingers, and a candle—two of them—at his head and candles at his feet—two of them. His mouth kept falling wide open and his brother, Little Prince, kept closing it, but since it wouldn't stay shut he would give up for a while and just wipe away the slobber that oozed from the corners of his mouth; then he would try again to push the lower jaw against the upper jaw hoping by some miracle it would stick—which of course it didn't. Outside, evening had come and I was hidden in darkness so they couldn't see me. For the people inside it was still day; the candles, some twenty of them that had lighted all the corners of the room since early morning, were burning with the same unchanging brightness, and it was their light that mattered to everybody there, not the time of day, and it was always the same brightness. Or maybe nothing mattered to them except Big Prince, and I was needlessly haunted by fears that they might catch a glimpse of me through the window, watching them. I knew that when you look at the sky from inside a room in the evening it looks blue, as in fact it is blue, as blue as snow, frozen and hard. I was propped up against the side of the house and the mulberry tree where Longbarrel's hens and turkeys roosted in the summer, and what had brought me here, over the fence and over the dogs, was the service of the dead that could be heard from the road, and the chilling mourning dirges sung by male voices, which were even more terrifying when someone would open the door of the house and the full sound would come pouring out. At Longbarrel's house no one could die except him, and I wouldn't have liked to see him dead, that man with no hair on his face who the women said was smaller than something he had that was bigger, an idea I hadn't been able to understand because he was barely as tall as the children in the fourth grade class. He wasn't the one who had died. I saw him as I came up to the window; he was on a three-legged chair next to the stove, stirring with a bayonet a pot of corn pudding that was on the fire. He came up next to Big Prince and, seeing that Little Prince couldn't get his mouth to stay shut, he went and with the tip of his bayonet stabbed a big red apple from among some quinces on top of the wardrobe, and went back without a word and tried to shove the apple into the dead man's mouth without taking it from the bayonet, and Little Prince got scared and pushed on the apple and it came off in his hand and he stood there laughing like an idiot. Longbarrel took the apple from his hand, with his own hand, and put it in the dead man's mouth and everybody laughed for a moment, maybe thinking about the roasted pigs that are brought to the table on a tray with an apple in their mouth. Then no one laughed anymore and Bitza's voice continued the dirge, hoarsely and somewhat nasally, reading from the palms of her hands, with her little fingers pushed together and her hands opened out in front of her eyes like a book. All the men said "Lord have mercy upon us," and Bitza looked first at one hand, her left, then at the other, her right, as if she were looking at two written pages and said: "Almighty God, You who have passed beyond death and Who have overthrown the devil, grant rest to the soul of Your departed servant, Prince John, in a place of light, in a luminous place, in a quiet and sweet place, in a place of green from which pain

has fled, from which grief and sighing have fled. . . ."
Then all the men said: "Lord have mercy upon us, the
priest catches fish for breakfast"—and I jumped in surprise. They couldn't have said "the priest catches fish for
breakfast;" they said . . . only up to those words that I,
that surely only I, could have said, in my own mind. But I
thought them, and so hard, that I even heard them. All
the children used to chant those words stupidly, and I
used to chant them too, but now it was absolutely dis-
graceful to repeat them. What horrified me more than the
words, or maybe this was why the words terrified me so
much, were the eyes of the dead man: they opened up and
looked at me exactly at the moment I heard: "The priest
catches fish for breakfast." The bitter cold began to make
the snow quiver as it sparkled faintly under the sickly,
almost dead light of the candles that filtered through the
window and the curtains. The snow got bumpy like goose
skin because of the cold that licked my ears and my nose
like a rabid bitch, making my teeth chatter frantically.
Longbarrel speared a coiled-up pork sausage with his bayonet and put it on the table next to Prince's left ear (he
even pushed his head a little to the right, with his elbow
so as not to soil his hands), and he cut it into pieces and
everyone took a piece of the sausage that was still siz-
zling, burning their fingers, and started to eat. Then I
noticed that between the dead man's outspread feet there
were some glasses. They filled them with hot wine from a
blue metal pot that had been placed next to the big pot of
corn pudding, clicked glasses with each other and drank,
dancing around the dead man and singing. This time I
knew I wasn't wrong. They said "the priest catches fish
for breakfast!" Pecker went out on the porch and then
came back in with two dead rabbits in his hands and one
around his neck like a fur. With the ones in his hands,
which he was holding by the tails, he started censing like
a priest around the dead man's head. I thought I was
dreaming so I rubbed my hands and beat my chest; I
wasn't dreaming, I was awake, but the cold had numbed

me and I was having hallucinations, and to stop hallucinating and keep from turning into an icicle, I left for home. I was, as usual, on stilts. Near the house the snow had melted some time before, but all through Longbarrel's backyard there were a number of paths that had been beaten down by pigs and it wasn't a problem for me to walk there with my wooden legs four meters long. I couldn't get through the gate and, in fact, I never tried to get in or out that way, and now I got to the road by stepping over the fence. The pole I held in my hands (to balance myself a little when necessary and to protect myself from the dogs and to warn jokesters that I could get at them from up where I was and flatten their hats and their caps and their jokes) turned white with frost, and the nail I had driven into the base of it so that it would stick in the ice or frozen ground went into the packed snow on the road with almost a squeak. Back at home no one believed me when I told them what I had seen. They laughed at me. Lereu, the gypsy who had come to our house to drink a hot *tzuica* (plum brandy) with pepper, was playing the violin on one string and he didn't even bother to give me the time of day. I was sorry that I couldn't go into the house on stilts and that I was forced to listen to everybody while looking up from down below. I had started to walk around on stilts because of the mud and because some circus people on stilts had passed through our village and I was astounded that they could be so far from the ground and so far above us, all of us whose jaws dropped at the sight of the ribbons they pulled out of their noses and ears. I started out with two tree branches about as long as a shepherd's staff, and in time I reached the height where I am now and where I like it: at four meters above the ground. The room was stifling and I had to put up with the stink of putrid, damp socks and tobacco. And Lereu's breath stank so much I was absolutely amazed that he didn't suffocate on the stench that was coming out of him. Lereu used to cut wood for people, and he used to split plum logs for us too. Sensing that I was looking at him, he said, while playing more just for himself next to his glass:

"They'd been out hunting."

"Who?" I asked.

"They," answered Lereu. "Today is the day when, in the good old days, the king used to come here to hunt. That is to say, the king came only once. And since then, every year on this day people go hunting."

"Why?" I didn't understand.

"Because on this day hunting is forbidden."

"And then it wasn't forbidden?"

"It was, but the king broke the law, and he had the right to do it because he was a king."

"And so they have the right?"

"They don't, but they break the law because they want to feel like kings. And on this day they are kings," said Lereu. "So, those guys are enjoying themselves like the kings and the emperors of the whole world."

"But they killed Prince . . . Or he might have just died," I corrected myself.

"It does happen," answered Lereu. "When the king came a man died then too . . . He was shot . . . He was a beater, or maybe he wasn't, no one knows for sure . . . Just as no one knows for sure if the one who came hunting here and who said he was the king was really the king, or if he was someone else . . . No one had ever seen the king either before or after that . . . Neither that one nor any other King."

I knew that Lereu wasn't quite right in the head, but I knew just as well that no one could top him in fabricating stories and I liked the story about the hunt that the king came to and I waited for it to go on, ready even to endure all the stench of his rotten teeth, which he tried in vain to wash off with hot *tzuica*—sweetened and peppered. Lereu fell silent and I saw my folks smiling at me on the sly; did they think that the gypsy was taking me in? But I, myself agreed to being taken in, and wanted him to take me in just for the pleasure of hearing how he could make up such incredible lies out of nothing.

"Prince is dead," I said trying to loosen his tongue.

"He isn't dead, because if he was they would have called that woman."

Then he nodded toward the lighted window that you could see from our window; there at Ostrogoth's, our neighbor on the hill, was a young nurse from Turnuvechi who was his tenant, and you could see through her lighted window with no curtains on it that she was at home; she was "that woman." Her name was Miss Florentine Firulescu. Every evening before going to bed she put newspapers up over the windows so that no one could see her when she got into bed. From the window of our room you could get a full view of her, and all the while I wondered why she ruined the papers every evening since there was no one to see her except us who were her neighbors, and the people who stopped by our house, or who came to husk corn: from the road no one could see in, it was impossible, the window of Ostrogoth's house being almost right up against ours that faced his house. We were separated only by a wooden fence and by a strip of land just big enough to allow the water from the roof to drip down and wash away the filth of everybody who squatted there at night so as not to freeze out at the back of the garden or out beyond the stable.

"If I say Prince is dead, he's dead," I started in again so as to get Lereu going once more.

"He's not dead, maybe just drunk . . . or maybe playing dead."

Lereu was drunk himself and couldn't lie any more as I would have liked. Prince had no reason to play dead; he would have gotten up when they put the apple in his mouth or would have gotten tired of staying stretched out on the table, surrounded by candles, while the others sang around him. And if he were pretending, then they had to be pretending too, but they weren't laughing, they were crying. Little Prince naturally knew who killed his brother, if someone did kill him and if he hadn't died from some illness or ended his own life with a bullet.

"Look, look!" I jumped up on the bed and urged them to look inside Ostrogoth's house.

Over there the door had opened and Miss Florentine Firulescu got up and left on the bed the book that she had been holding on her knees and talked to somebody we couldn't see. Was that "somebody" talking through the half-open door? Nobody paid any attention to me, but I didn't let their indifference bother me: I knew they couldn't believe I was in my right mind since I had started going around on stilts (just as I couldn't believe Lereu wasn't cracked)—especially when they started beating me to try to stop me from walking through the village like a stork and then realized that their beatings didn't do any good. The door closed, but Miss Firulescu stayed where she was and kept on talking. Was she talking to someone who was outside the door? Or was she talking to herself? She was talking to herself because she began walking back and forth in the room, first toward one wall, then toward the other, and never shut up. Was she reciting poetry? I thought of going outside and getting up on my stilts next to her window to see better when, standing up on my tiptoes I saw a cap moving next to her bed, a cap that seemed to be floating. And I started to laugh. Nobody wore a green hunter's cap in the winter except Longbarrel. That's who it was, that damn dwarf. Miss Firulescu put her coat over her shoulders, blew out the lamp and went out the door holding a lantern in front of her so that Longbarrel could see his way and not trip on the stairs. So, Prince did die. Even the condition Lereu demanded to accept his death was fulfilled: to have that woman called. Longbarrel had called her. (I didn't understand why they called him Longbarrel when he was, in fact, named Longland. That's how it was written on his wagon: Longland, John. Patirlagele district, village of Braniste). I looked at my folks and at Lereu with tremendous pride: I had been

right. Prince had died! There wasn't any point in talking
to them any more: I went out, got up on my stilts, which I
had left stuck in the straw in the shed, and took off in the
dark for Longbarrel's house. I went through yards, over
fences and got to the window where I had stood earlier,
before the master of the house and the nurse had come
through the gate. Longbarrel had short legs and took tiny
steps—so that before he arrived I heard Bitza again singing nasally at the head of the dead man:

"For You . . . You created Prince from dust and
light . . . And You formed him and gave him his name,
and his voice and his strength . . . And now You have
undone this unspoken tie and the man formed by You
from earth and light will dissolve into earth and light,
into those things out of which You brought him into
being . . ."

I wasn't cold anymore, I had also taken Lereu's sheep-
skin coat that had been left out on the porch. There
wasn't any question anymore of seeing ghosts because of
the cold; with all that, nothing had changed in the house;
all the men were drinking hot wine, and Pecker had
brought, in the meantime a pot full of sauerkraut in brine
which, what can I say, made every one of them happy . . .
Only Prince, with the red apple in his mouth, didn't move
off the table . . . When Longbarrel (Longland) arrived with
Miss Firulescu, there was a moment of silence; my hope
that the whole matter was going to be cleared up warmed
me considerably, just as if I had drunk their hot wine.
Miss Florentine Firulescu went over to the dead man, felt
for his pulse on his left hand and then whispered something to Longbarrel and nodded to him. He went and took
a blanket from the bed and covered up the window that
looked out onto the road. Some marvel was about to occur before my eyes, something that shouldn't be witnessed by anyone. My happiness melted quickly; Longbarrel also put up a blanket on the window where I was. I
could see only the light from the candles coming dimly
through the thick woven wool. Not a single hole nor rip

was in that blanket. The hope that, for a few moments in my imagination, had taken the shape of a rip—and that's really what it can be called—died. The only thing I had left was my hearing. However, in a house where hot wine is on the stove and a dead man is lying on the table, you can't tell, if you can't see, what is really truly true. Even before, when I could see their faces, I didn't get anything at all out of their words. I heard them suddenly burst out laughing. Or burst out crying, I don't know which. I moved away from the window, and all around dogs barked seeing me go over the fences like a shadow. That kind of mixture of laughter and tears I had heard some time before, one summer, and Lereu hearing it at that time too, had said: "They're having fun." Which seemed dumb to me. I was with Gicu, my cousin, he on foot and I on stilts. The whole village was coming back from work in wagons and carts. The dust made their faces look paler. The sand blown by the wind from Serbia got into their shirts and into their skin. Motionless, swung by the wheels, numbed by the weariness that had come from a day of reaping, they looked asleep. And if it hadn't been for their round, bright eyes, you would have thought that the oxen and horses were bringing back to the village their masters who had been killed by the sun that had shone on them since morning as they bent over to cut the wheat and tie it in sheaves. A long funeral procession flowing toward the village. And the dust continuously raised by the hooves of the first horses and dragged along by the hooves of the oxen and run over by the front wheels of the wagons then seemed to be thrown up again and mixed with the breath and the horseshoes of the animals who were harnessed and yoked to the line of wagons, and moved along like a cloud that was sometimes gray, sometimes reddish over the heads of the people, making them look like earthen people trying to get into the village. And the animals who were drawing what looked like an endless monster on ungreased wheels, they too resembled earthen horses and oxen. And you didn't know afterwards, just as when you're drunk, if they went forward through the horrible dust on the road, crazed from the days without rain of that summer, or if a dry, stifling, black cloud had passed over the heads of some earthen creatures, and since it would seem to move away and then not to move, it would uncover them, but not too much, and let them be seen. When they reached the bend in the road, near the Danube, a few hundred feet from the village where, during the day, the geese fed and the children played stick ball, the wagons stopped as if on some signal and the people emerged from the dust as if from a cloak and went toward the willow trees beside the water and began, the men a little ways downstream and the women further upstream, to throw off their clothes and to jump into the Danube head first, or to walk in slowly, feeling with each step how the water soaked into their flesh with its old madness. The children unharnessed the horses and went into the Danube riding on the horses' backs further downstream, where the oxen were led to get watered and washed. People and animals together washed away the dust and went into the village shining and fresh, and in any case appearing younger. On that kind of evening, after the bathing in the river, I saw for myself what soldiers were like. About ten of them appeared in view coming from Bistretz. I saw them first but it was Gicu who told me: "Those are soldiers." They were holding a dozen geese that had been shot. Exactly twelve, I counted them three times. They went in single file, quietly, so quietly that not one of the people who had been bathing in the Danube noticed them. They kept going straight toward the village, along the path. I took off after them, along with everybody else, and I wasn't frightened of their rifles or their helmets but of their faces; I felt a kind of fear too of the geese carried by the neck in their hands, or with their heads stuffed under belts. That evening I saw them in Pecker's yard, boiling the geese in a cauldron used for making soap. The next day a few more came and they ate what was left of the meal the others had. They put the cauldron on the fire, and then four of them took it by the handle and set it on some big logs; then they climbed up on those logs, and got around the cauldron, and started to eat from it, each with his own spoon as if they were at a village funeral dinner. Going upstream on the Danube there were boats, and there was a booming from all kinds of guns, and all kinds of soldiers of all kinds of ranks who spoke all kinds of languages were coming and going. What I want to say has to do with Lereu's "They're having fun." Well, one evening, some of the soldiers ate in Pecker's yard again—he also had a cauldron used for boiling plum jam—a kind of soup made with boiled wheat. I had no idea what country they came from, they could have even been our own people, I didn't know what a nation was at that time; I only saw that they ate, and burst into laughter, or some of them looked as if they had burst into tears. Before long they would laugh as if, as Lereu said: "They're having fun."

"What are they doing?" I asked from up on my stilts.

"They're joking around," Lereu answered.

He always said such dumb things, that gypsy. I actually felt sorry for them until the day they brought some prisoners with them who, in fact, looked just like them except that they had different clothes on. They kept them in Gicu's bed for three days and three nights, naked.

"Is that how they have to be kept?" Gicu asked Lereu.

"They're joking around," answered Lereu.

And from then on I was convinced that he was the only man with the strength of a man left in the village. On a Sunday, a prisoner said something, beating on the wall with his chained fists, and a soldier dragged him out of bed and gave him back his clothes and went off to the Danube with him, toward Bistretz. There, by the willows, where in the summer the people coming home from the fields get undressed, he said something to the prisoner and the prisoner got undressed. "Ah ha," I said to myself, "he asked if he could wash." The prisoner, naked, bathed himself, and the soldier held his clothes and his watch.

The prisoner didn't know how to swim, and splashed around right next to the shore and kept watching the man on the shore with ice-cold eyes. I was there without my stilts, in a nearby poplar tree, with Gicu. Then, when he had had enough of the water, he came toward the shore, holding his hand in front of what a man has that is his, somehow ashamed. When he was about five steps from the shore, he tripped in the sand. That's what I thought. But then I heard. He let his hand fall down from his things, as if puzzled, then fell to his knees. The water had been up to his knees and now it reached his neck. He tried to drag himself to the shore, but then started as if bitten on the neck by a rabid dog, and I saw him writhing about with his head down, as if he had forgotten that the ground was downward and what you put on it is your feet, and that you don't go on it with your head . . . He glided down the Danube, like a sheep swollen with water. The guy on the shore flung the clothes into the Danube and kept only the watch. All night long I swore at Lereu, then and now. Then, when I woke up, I saw Ostrogoth's wife shaking out some red blankets from her window. Now, when I woke up, at Ostrogoth's open window stood Big Prince eating sunflower seeds and talking to Miss Firulescu. I had seen a man who was risen from the dead, and there was nothing left in life for me to see. "If you see a man die and then see one rise from the dead, you have nothing more in the world left to see," Lereu had said to me that summer. "There is no other miracle."

Lereu didn't know anything. From that very morning when I saw Big Prince alive, I stayed in bed until the leaves had come out on Ostrogoth's locust tree, where the stork had its nest. I slept wrapped in cloths soaked in *tzuica*, and I kept seeing the people at Longbarrel's singing around the dead man, who was lying amidst the candles. The cold penetrated all my bones. And it wouldn't go away except when it wanted to. Miss Florentine pierced me to no avail with her boiled needles.

"What's she doing?" I heard Mama ask Lereu one day while he was drinking his ration of *tzuica*.

"She's having fun."

As for me, I wasn't scared of dying, but I was afraid of the heat that made me delirious at night so that I kept seeing soldiers eating geese, and rows of prisoners coming out of the Danube, each covering his privates with his hand. And I was especially terrified by the red blanket that I saw in my dreams covering everything and getting closer and closer to my eyelids to blind me, and to my lips so as to cut off all the air from my mouth and suffocate me. And in my sleep, all of Longbarrel's dogs would come out in front of me, and his neighbors' dogs who had barked at me that night when I saw Prince dead. I was swimming in dirty water, and on the right bank there were dogs with silver teeth waiting for me, and on the left, bitches with gold teeth. I was afraid of sleep in the evening; afraid of the dogs in my dreams. Afraid of the red blanket. And even worse than the dogs, I was afraid of the people in my dreams: Longbarrel had two heads, in front the head of a man and in back the head of a dog, and he barked. And Pecker's neck held up two heads. And both the Princes barked like dogs too. And Bitza had dog's teeth in her human mouth, and in her bitch's mouth, human teeth that were gilded. With one head they talked and with the other they snarled, sang and yelped all at the same time, and they turned somersaults or played leap-frog, and when they got hungry they'd go and eat a soldier who was coming out of the water, alive and naked. And they came to me to grind me between their teeth, but my luck was in my stilts: they couldn't reach me. However, one night Pecker started to dig around my stilts, and as they sank slowly into the ground as if in a bog, I saw those monsters' eyes growing bigger. I was getting closer to them the closer to the ground I got.

"Mama!" I screamed and woke up, wet in every possible way, and soaking in all my water.

My folks slapped me on the cheeks to make me open my eyes, and when I opened them I saw great relief in their faces; as if I had come back from the dead.

"What did you dream?" they asked me.

And I told them everything while they rubbed me down with vinegar from head to foot. But when I went back to sleep, the dream continued where it had left off: men with heads of a man and a dog ate some more naked soldiers. I saw them eat a man with one mouth and with the other spit out the bones. I was still slipping into the ground, Pecker was digging hurriedly. I was in the monsters' realm and when I screamed "Mama" again and woke up, slapped lightly on the face by my folks, I breathed with relief, but I wasn't waking up from death as my folks thought, I wasn't being raised from the dead; no. The monsters weren't dead creatures; I had apparently been in their world, in the land of people who eat people. No, I hadn't died. And I told my folks:

"I didn't die at all, I swear! I fell into a bad dream."

And something had to be done so that I wouldn't fall into it again, so I wouldn't see those eaters of human flesh, so I wouldn't hear them bark. They called Baba Sevastitza to take the spell off me so that I wouldn't dream about Pecker digging under my stilts. Sevastitza brought hair from Pecker's head. She burned to ashes the hair she had brought and she broke the spell that was on me; and I didn't dream about Pecker anymore. Then one morning I heard a lot of racket, with men talking and dogs barking. I woke up, or maybe I hadn't been sleeping, I don't know for sure. I felt even more afraid. I wasn't soaked with sweat, my ears weren't buzzing, my bones didn't ache and not my body either, I could see the sun, warm and soft, coming in the open window, so I must have been all there; but still, the mixed sounds of the voices of men and the barking of dogs filled the whole house and seemed to fill the whole backyard and the whole village. I plugged up my ears with my fingers, hard, but I'm not sure if I heard them grow any weaker. I gave a start: those sounds didn't come from inside of me, they weren't mine. I took my fingers out of my ears, and since I was alone in the house, I tried to get out of bed to see if I was hallucinating or not. My legs held me. I felt lighter, my sickness seemed to have taken me back a couple of years. I went out, supporting myself against the house, and I got to the gate. Everything became clear: on the road, walking toward the forest with their dogs on leash, were the hunters. Among them were Pecker, Longbarrel and the Princes. But they didn't have two heads anymore.

It was then I was sure that the sickness had left me. Or that it had died in me, by itself, as Baba Sevastitza had muttered that it would, I don't know. That afternoon I wolfed down everything they put in front of me, like a gypsy. So, the men had gone hunting. What they were hunting I didn't know and I didn't care either. To go hunting, the hunt itself is what matters, they say, and what falls under the rifle is of almost no importance. The pleasure of hunting is the only thing that counts, I found out later. I, myself, couldn't know their pleasure in it, there in the fields or in the forest where they went to look for wolves or foxes or God knows what. But I had seen, on their faces, the pleasure they had as they went out with their dogs on leash. Much more than the rifle (a dead thing against their backs like a stake), chubby dogs or dogs with a long muzzle or with legs as long as staffs were the pride of their masters. Longbarrel had christened his mastiff Caesar; Cowskinner, Mussolini; Pecker had dubbed his Franz Joseph. While eating I thought of all the dogs who had gone out of the village: Napoleon, Peter, Phillip, Hitler, William, Henry, King (Big Prince's dog), Leopold, Richard (Little Prince's dog), Joseph [Stalin], Alexander . . . I knew from Lereu that all the dogs in our village had the names of kings or emperors. And I got to laughing, while eating, remembering how the hunters swaggered along like children, all puffed up because they could order around a dog who had a king's name. At least this way they could feel above history, I thought later, as I remembered this scene, history that was more horrifying than just a few dogs with lofty names, whom they could love and whose fur they could caress, or whom they could get to go after rabbits or foxes, or purely and simply, whom they could kill if need be. I'll never forget how in the middle of all the hunters was (the only one on horseback) Galatioan, who had moved to Cimpuletz several years before. He was the only one without a dog, and precisely because of that, it seemed to me that he was haughtier than all the other hunters; in any case, he had a glint in his eye, as if all the hunters were really his dogs.

Toward evening they came noisily back, covered with dirt, pretty drunk, and without dogs. They had let them go on home when they sat down with their food and drink at the edge of the forest, around the body of the wolf that had been shot. The dogs hadn't gotten lost. Now they came out on the heels of their masters, fawning on them. Galatioan was walking too, and on the horse where he had sat that morning, draped over the saddle, the wolf dangled, dead, with its tongue hanging out and with its legs all limp, like strips of cloth. Longbarrel gave his Caesar a swift kick in the stomach to get him into his backyard, and Ostrogoth did the same to his bitch, Caesarina. And while everyone was laughing at the yelps of a mastiff, huge and shaggy as a wolf the way Caesar was, they saw—and I saw too from the gate—Pecker's Franz Joseph coming toward the horse like a blind creature, about to walk between its legs. Pecker gave him a kick in the ribs too, and Franz Joseph fell on his ass, but got up immediately, as if he didn't even notice that his master had beaten him, and continued on his way toward the horse as if drunk. Pecker struck him again, and then it was obvious that Franz Joseph hadn't even felt the first blow, because he didn't feel the second one either, which meant that he was so drunk he couldn't even feel pain.

"Whatever did you give him to drink?"

"Me, hell . . . Maybe the children at home teased him and poured *tzuica* down his throat . . ."

"Smell him, maybe he reeks of wine."

Pecker yelled to him, but Franz Joseph didn't respond; he just rubbed his snout in the dirt of the road as he walked along, getting himself all covered with dust. And everybody started to roar with laughter, especially when the animal, as if trying to entertain them, wiped his snout with his paw. The hunters gathered around him, and since they were drunk, they lifted him up in their arms to smell his snout and everybody shouted that it stank of the bottle. Then they all started pushing him around with their feet, from one person to another, like a ball, without actually kicking him, and dying with laughter. And from so much rolling around in the dust, the dog just lay there with his tail between his legs, and when he barked, he barked a hoarse, *tzuica* bark, with a sound that was all different, and he seemed to be trying to play and snap at them in fun, but didn't have the strength. His bark made the men hold their bellies from so much laughing. And then I saw Lereu going up to the dog and shouting:

"Stop, are you crazy, can't you see he's rabid?"

"How could my dog be rabid, you scum?" Pecker shouted rudely at him. "He's drunk," he laughed.

"He's rabid, can't you see how he's foaming at the mouth, and how he's got red eyes?"

They all looked at Franz Joseph, taking a step backwards, and didn't laugh anymore. And they stepped aside when the dog got up out of the dirt, stiff as a board, and tried to go on his way—and I heard them load their guns, and all the rifles seemed to go off at the same time, and the dog died without ever hearing anything; he fell with his legs pointing up, struck and turned over on his back by the bullets, without ever feeling any pain.

My legs got strong again and I was able to go around freely on stilts, a sure sign that I had escaped from the days of lying in bed, and the sick nights when the man-eaters gradually looked more and more like my neighbors and people I knew. That freak of a Longbarrel had turned himself into an ogre too, a dwarf ogre; the head in front was Longland's, and the one in back was Caesar's. At night, in my dreams, every neighbor lived in the same body with his dog, and it was amazing that I never dreamed about Lereu. Maybe because he didn't have a dog. All my dreams vanished when I started going around on stilts again. In the evening I'd fall flat into bed and sleep like a rock until morning. The storks came, and the swallows, and rebuilt their old nests, and I was the only person who could look inside their nests whenever I wanted. I was above their nests, which at times strengthened my conviction that when a person dies, he too becomes a bird, a swallow or a stork, and comes to make his nest under the eaves or on top of the house he had as a man. On top of my wooden legs, high up, even the air was sweeter, the dust was finer and scarcer, and people's voices were softer, and their eyes smaller. They looked at me with their faces turned up to the sky, the same way they looked up at clouds or birds. I had separated myself from them, living four meters above them, as isolated as if I were in another village, or another world. Neither dogs, nor men, nor mud, nor rabies could get up to where I was. For, after they had killed Franz Joseph, they hit seven more dogs on the head with clubs or axes, dogs with hanging jaws who were miserable and hoarse, and who had run away from home. The summer heat came early, heavy, unbearable, without a breath of wind and without any rainy skies. The flies multiplied and it began to stink in the backyards from the garbage that wasn't burned in the fall or taken to the fields in the spring. Leaves that had barely come out in the morning would droop around noon, and the leaves on the pumpkins and the sorrel would melt like wax and flop down on the ground as if they wanted to die. Dogs kept on leash in shady places were forever shuffling around the water put out in pans for them to drink, and barking and snapping at the flies that swarmed around them as if they were dead. Or maybe they indeed smelled like the dead; the Unseen was at work inside of them, as Lereu said. The water in the wells began to dry up and people, looking ahead, gathered up the straw and hay and cornstalks that were left over from the past winter, with an eye to the winter to come. Miss

Florentine Firulescu walked around with a bag in which she had a syringe with poison in it, and the dogs, picked up on the road by the groups of voluntary dogcatchers she organized, were led into a pen in the back of the clinic and, without any regard for whether they were sick or healthy, they were injected on the spot. I myself saw the voluntary dogcatchers, as that same Lereu called them, never sober, having "fun": that is, I saw how they did their catching. They each had some kind of wire noose, and when they found a dog on the road, they went and waited for him right at his gate or at a hole in the fence, and the dog was chased with stones and hooted at from one side to the other until he put his head into the ring that choked him and subdued him; the more he struggled, the more he tried to get loose, the faster he passed out. Pecker had become an unsurpassed dogcatcher, and his eagerness to rid the village of stray dogs was really more a desire to exterminate other people's dogs too. When he caught Bodea's bitch next to the school, Bodea was in his backyard and saw it, but he didn't say anything: he knew that Miss Florentine would have had the dog taken into the pen, and on top of that, he could have been fined. But more than anything, he was afraid that his bitch might somehow have gotten sick too, by breaking the chain and going out onto the road. It was better not to have a dog around the house, it was safer. Yes, yes, it was safer. You could see in Bodea's eyes that he liked what he saw, as if once his bitch was gone, the rabies he so feared would be gone too, and any possiblity of ever getting diseased would be warded off for him and for his family. He ran down into his cellar and came back with a bottle of *tzuica*. But he just stood there with it in his hand. No one would have thought that he wanted to pay them for killing his bitch. He did want to, and still wanted to: it was better if they killed her, otherwise he could have had to hit her on the head himself. He had raised her from a pup and felt a kind of pity for her. He was, in a word, happy that the dogcatchers were killing her. He drank alone from the bottle, and poured out a few drops for the soul of the dead creature—who, however, hadn't yet died.

I caught up with the dogcatchers next to the clinic. And I noticed that they were waiting for something impatiently. Catching dogs was a kind of game, a sort of joke of a hunt. It didn't give them any satisfaction; they knew the dogs weren't stricken with rabies; when they were catching them in their noose, they had no fear of the dogs. And because they had no fear, they didn't get any fun out of it. That's why they waited silently for the moment when Miss Florentine would fill her syringe with the horrible serum. There, certain death was to be found, in phials lined up in rows in little cardboard boxes; and death flowed from the little, long-necked bottles into the syringe. And Miss Florentine held the syringe in her right hand with the needle pointing up, and made for the dogs immobilized in the pen. This time there were about twenty of them, shaggy dogs, sheep dogs, young males, two white puppies, and Bodea's bitch. The syringe pricked each of them and its effect could be seen right away. The legs of some of them began to weaken, their eyes began to cloud over and then to darken. And only then did I understand what the dogcatchers were waiting for: they were waiting to see how good and how fast death was at doing its job.

And for all their being hunters and thick-skinned, when they found themselves facing twenty corpses from which life had departed but that still had warmth in them and were still kicking, they forgot where they were and took their hats off their heads, as if faced with a human death.

Florentine went into the clinic, and they were still under the spell that had felled the dogs, were still stupefied and a bit horrified, but all the same proud of having seen what devastating power could be contained in a few little bottles, and be held in Miss Firulescu's right hand, and be unleashed ruthlessly and indiscriminately . . . They saw, yes saw, death itself, how it came and settled forever in living flesh. They were staring at how the dogs lay motionless, silent, and would have stayed like that longer if a shaggy dog hadn't barked, terrified of them and terrified of those that had not yet begun to stink, except to his nostrils, there in the pen. Cowskinner swatted at him with his hat and ran after him with his wire noose to catch him, but Longbarrel grabbed him by the arm and stopped him.

"That's *his* dog . . ." said Big Prince.

"What a handsome dog, and so strong," Ostrogoth said flatteringly.

"Here boy, here boy," Pecker called to him, and searched through his pack and felt sorry when he couldn't find any food to give him.

The shaggy dog jumped over a fence and went about his affairs in Milksop's garden, and then went out onto the road once more, next to Bodea's house. I saw him again toward evening, going through gardens and wandering around freely everywhere. The dogcatchers didn't touch him the next day either, and the day after that, Pecker, when he met up with him, pulled a big chunk of bread out of his pack and threw it to him. This time he hadn't forgotten to take bread with him. The shaggy dog ate it up and Ostrogoth said, with a great deal of pleasure, and loudly so that everyone could hear:

"How nicely he eats, guys, just like a human."

A week later Milksop's daughter died, for reasons unknown, and they all thought that she had been bitten by some rabid dog. A young doctor, Danila, came out from Turnuvechi and said that the girl had died of pneumonia. Danila stayed on in Braniste, which meant that he had been appointed to a position here and hadn't made the trip just to see Milksop's dead girl. Three widows wanted to take him in as a lodger but, not knowing that they were widows, he didn't go to any of those three houses. He wanted to be near the clinic. After a few days he found a room at Bodea's, and they came to an agreement on the price. When they were alone in the room together, Bodea asked him in a whisper:

"Didn't she have rabies?"

"No . . . Why?" laughed Danila.

"Because they killed a pile of dogs . . . because we had rabies come into the village . . ."

And he told him how the dogcatchers had taken his bitch too and had killed her. And how not a single animal—ox, sheep, goat, or horse, or anything else—had the right to go around in the village without its master, so that it wouldn't get bitten by some rabid dog. And how all the dogs were tied up in their yards so that they wouldn't by some chance spread the disease, if they were afflicted with it. Danila laughed and looked out the open window.

"Nonsense," said Danila. "That there, isn't that a dog?"

The shaggy dog stopped in front of the clinic and relieved himself with his left hind leg lifted up against a telephone pole.

"That's . . ." Bodea laughed.

"It's what?"

"It's *his* . . . I mean his parent's, since he's in Cimpuletz. It's still his though, since it's theirs."

"And him they don't . . . ?"

"Well . . . You know . . . It's *his* . . ."

"To hell with the damn dog, screw him!" Danila got infuriated and went out into the village, and when he met up with Florentine and found out from her that they had killed so many dogs that were supposedly rabid, he said:

"Milksop's girl had rabies."

"I knew it," said Pecker.

"You didn't want to scare people," said Longbarrel.

"Or to make her father angry . . . Now that she's in her grave . . ."

"We won't tell anyone . . ."

"All loose dogs . . . you understand?" Danila asked them.

"Absolutely," answered Pecker.

"No exceptions," continued Danila.

"Of course," stressed Big Prince.

"Let's go," proposed Danila, and they all followed him gravely. And for three hours straight they rounded up dogs, but they didn't come across the shaggy dog. The only thing the doctor wanted was to find that one. Danila was the only one who knew the truth about the death of Milksop's girl—she had died of pneumonia, and absolutely not of rabies—but what interested him was not that truth, but another that seemed even more horrifying to him. Toward evening they came upon the russet-colored shaggy dog, and when Danila told them to catch him, they grinned. And they didn't touch the dog. Thus, he had lied to them in vain, he told Lereu later, because he couldn't make them catch the russet dog. Or maybe not in vain, since he had found out something: that there was a thing they feared more than rabies. That is to say, there was a disease more horrible than rabies.

2

It was something to see, how every morning Florentine opened her window up wide, and then went out into the backyard to the well and filled the trough with water and, almost naked, washed herself. And it was quite another thing to realize that she wasn't doing it for me, just a crazy kid at that time (and what I saw then I understand only now, or I understood in the meantime, listening to what others who were older had understood). And that she wasn't doing it for Longbarrel, that dwarf born out of his own maleness, who would come with sleep in his eyes and hide in the corncobs around Ostrogoth's shed so as not to miss the light—as he stammered out in confession to his friends—the the light of Miss Florentine's legs, of her breasts, and of her back as the water, struck by the rising sun, refreshed her. And not for the benefit of the gossip tongues did she start her morning whistling, nor even for Danila, who had moved to our house—to watch over my health and because he didn't like the food at Bodea's. And not for anyone else's benefit did she go out into the yard barefooted and dressed in her birthday suit. She didn't do it for anybody or anything. She was beautiful, and I could say—to use one of Danila's expressions—shamefully beautiful and shamefully happy, because she thought only of herself and of her body, and the washing and the walk through the yard in the morning were nothing other than a natural, elemental act, performed by her and for her alone, like a kind of prayer that she sent up to her own body, the only altar in any case that she would bow before.

That was Danila's conclusion. At first he, too, believed that she was a bit eccentric, or that she acted like that to irritate the men who had been waiting there so long for her, so as to be able to prolong and increase it all tenfold with their own fantasies. But even their slander was of no interest to Florentine. She was so serious that Danila, who at first watched her, pretending that he was shaving on the porch and couldn't see her, never actually shaved at all: he purely and simply watched her and admired her. At the beginning I made the mistake of thinking that he was only looking at that light mentioned by Longbarrel. Until he told me, or rather, told Lereu:

"It's incredible how blind she is."

"What do you mean, blind?"

"Well, she doesn't see anyone until she's dressed and goes out into the village; absolutely no one, that's why she doesn't care. And she doesn't see because she doesn't think about anything except herself."

"And the people who see her.?"

"It doesn't matter to her if anyone sees her or not: they'er all just stones, just sticks; in other words they don't exist!"

I didn't understand anything at that time, and judging from the way he scratched his face under his beard, neither did Lereu.

"Which means?" Lereu probed him.

"Which means that she doesn't love anyone."

"Yes, that sounds right," said Lereu, "so it didn't do you any good to move from Bodea's."

"Pardon me?" said Danila.

"Nothing," continued Lereu. "She's blind, that young woman, she's blind."

And the gypsy tittered at me with his metal teeth, and I was horrified and grimaced, not because of Danila's incredible discovery that she was blind (I didn't believe it one little bit and didn't understand what he meant), not because of Lereu's joke in which he took me as an accomplice, I grimaced purely and simply sensing—although he was at some distance and it didn't reach me—the putrid stench of Lereu's teeth. However much good that man had in him, I couldn't stand to get near him for that reason. And, cross my heart, I was more fond of him than of seven or seventeen or I don't know how many people who didn't have skin as dark as his, and whose shirts didn't stink of smoke. The smoke that walked around with him, embedded in his skin, in his hair and in his clothes, didn't sicken me. Only the mouth. Baba Sevastitza once told him: "Your mouth stinks of all the sins that have come out of it." It was a dumb thing to say; it didn't have anything to do with sins, but with rotten teeth.

"So, we can look at her openly," said Lereu; "she's blind and doesn't see us."

"Right," agreed Danila. "But these blind, selfish, sleep-walking beasts don't like to be awakened."

"What would she do, bite?"

"Maybe."

"Who's afraid of a woman who bites?" laughed the gypsy. And when Danila had left for the clinic, Lereu asked me: "Did you see how red the doctor's ears were?"

"Yes, why?"

"He says that they got sunburned . . . She burned his ears, that's why." And he left me wondering.

I went back to watching Florentine (my folks had left for work and so had everyone at Ostrogoth's) and it didn't seem to me that she couldn't see: she put the soap back in exactly the same place she took it from, in an empty boot cream box which Ostrogoth had fastened to the wooden post of the well. Then I heard, from near the barn, the rustling of a big rat: Longbarrel was coming out from the corncobs and was leaving for home. Florentine went into the house and it was all over for him. Ostrogoth had a high fence made of wide planks; you couldn't see into his yard from the road. And not anywhere near his well; between the well and the road was the kitchen. Only from our house could you see everything at Ostrogoth's, just as from his place you could see our whole front yard. I left for the clinic too. I would have liked to see how a young nurse or medical assistant could be blind, and what it would be like when a man whose ears are burning for her (which is what Lereu meant, isn't it?) puts his hands on her and looks her in the eye. For me, at that time, it was all very clear: she pretended not to see anyone, even not to see Danila, to drive him to the looney hospital and show him that none of his learning was good for anything. As I heard Danila tell her with my own ears, against rabies you have to protect people and dogs before they're bitten and get the disease, because once it starts, it goes on hopelessly to death, and no medicine can stop its fatal advance, and no treatment exists, and rabies can't be defeated, it defeats everything that men know, it's above medicine and human knowledge: it's above us like death, Danila had said. And maybe Florentine wanted to show him that she, too, was above all his power and knowledge.

3

"Listen, Nicanor: what you're telling me is all very interesting, or interesting enough, so you won't think I'm trying to flatter you in some way or other. It's not only the facts you're telling me that seem worth remembering; I'm especially impressed by the way you choose these scenes that you lived through in childhood. How some people remained imprinted in your memory, how you try to show these people through a prism that is, so to speak, double; the way you understood things then and the way you're trying to understand them now and explain to yourself what you saw back in your childhood. But I, myself, am interested in something very precise, excuse me for interrupting you: I would like to find out, more exactly, what you know about Kalagherovich. It was about him that I asked you to tell me from the very beginning, what you had seen or heard about him, and so far you haven't even mentioned his name. Of course, the man is dead, and maybe it seems strange to you that I'm interested in a dead man. I'm still hoping that he isn't dead. Kalagherovich is no relative of yours or mine, and apparently back then, when he had the threat of death hanging over him, no one claimed him as a relative. Which isn't unusual: a condemned man loses his relatives without wanting to. So that they don't have to share, rightly or wrongly, in his fate. And yet, there was somebody who didn't betray him, otherwise you can't explain why he died or disappeared so much later. There was one witness who kept him alive—a relative who wasn't a blood relative, but who counted then for much more than a real family member. I like to think, myself, that my father was that man. It's just an opinion, or maybe something

else: an explanation for my father's death. One of several
explanations, perhaps. I want to get at Kalagherovich so
as, in fact, to get at my father's death. From what I've
found out, the man who wanted Kalagherovich's downfall
had no interest in my father's fate; in any case, he didn't
bear him any ill will. That he might not have wished him
well either doesn't count. It's merely a sign of indifference, not wishing someone well. The danger comes
when indifference disappears, and it only disappears in
darker cases. Kalagherovich, what was he? He didn't have
to be anything in order to be put down. His name gave
him an advantage for dying. He didn't even have his own
identity to help him. Everything was so arranged that
there was nothing for him to do but escape from what he
was accused of, or accept the charges brought against him
and either disappear or die. He refused to accept. You
sensed very well the psychology of the people in Braniste
who didn't have the nerve to touch Galatioan's dog.
Everybody admired (you noticed with the sensitivity of
your youth, which records every look faultlessly) the russet, shaggy dog and praised him as if Galatioan could
somehow hear them if they hit or slandered his dog. Or if
they cursed him. Who would insult his animal? I know
that his old folks also had some pigs who ate grape skins
every day at the hot *tzuica* cauldron, and no one chased
them away, not even after they were full and satisfied and
would lie down to sleep any old place. And they also had a
horse who would graze anywhere he happened to be. You
grasped very well how people can be humiliated in the
presence of animals belonging to certain individuals.
From this I deduce their attitude toward that individual:
not only were they humble, they were literally hypno-
tized, transformed, into what? In any case, into something deaf and blind, the way a shovel or a tool of some
kind has to be. I believe that it was on that fear of theirs of
the russet, shaggy dog that the whole strategy for Kalagherovich's liquidation was constructed by whoever the
interested party was. It would be interesting if you could

recall anyone in particular who passed through the village back then—besides Doctor Danila—who might have noticed the people's fear of the russet, shaggy dog. The fear, and the ridiculousness of that fear; because never would they have caught that dog in their noose, not even if he had been sick with rabies. It's hard for you to remember exactly what I would like you to, and maybe it's hopeless for me to attempt to discover, if not the truth, at least a thread of that truth based on your memories, on the impressions of the child, Nicanor, and on what has been preserved from those impressions by the Nicanor of the present. Many of the details of one's childhood slip away, but some fundamental images remain. They follow us all, like criminals or angels. Forgive me for that stupid comparison. What I wanted to say is that, however much we try to run away from them, however far we advance in years, they will still always be with us, their details will grow larger. I'm convinced that ten years from now, the soldier-prisoner who comes out of the water in your dreams and in moments of recall will become so real to you that you'll feel his breath and hear his last words and see the color of his eyes, and you'll tell it all. Everything back then that was clearly imprinted in you, but that was troubled by emotion, everything that you once tried to forget, or did forget without wanting to, will in time acquire for you its initial proportions, vivid and painful. And even if you now remembered something fundamental about Kalagherovich, I don't know if that something would constitute supporting evidence in the eyes of the law or of men: who would base his actions on memories, on impressions? Everybody wants only concrete details, material, palpable proofs. My attempt might appear doomed from the outset. That may be so. But even if I don't discover what I want, that particular truth, the atmosphere that made that truth possible would have been uncovered. I've discussed the years and the days I'm interested in with a great number of other people. I've come to a conclusion that I'm going to tell you before asking

you to go on with your story. Here it is: Kalagherovich
was the main target, but he didn't die first, or didn't disappear first. I found myself, I believe, faced with an interesting hypothesis and with an intelligent type of criminal,
one who is thus quite extraordinary. The target therefore—Kalagherovich. But there were several witnesses
who knew that Kalagherovich would have to disappear or
at least who sensed it. Some of them were asked to collab-
orate directly, others only to provide testimony more
criminal than the crime itself, because that crime of
theirs would be based, calmly and serenely, and rightly in
everybody's eyes, on that testimony. And the one interested in doing away with Kalagherovich, before wiping
him out, did something unimaginable: he did away with
the witnesses. Here are my conclusions: when Kalagherovich died, not one witness was still alive. A per-
fect crime, one that could be written up in a textbook.
And that's the way it was. The only ones still alive now,
unless they died of some disease or for some other reason,
are Kalagherovich's assassins. And you. Or more precisely: you and your memory. I got the idea of asking you
to tell me about this man a few days ago, when you told
me in the cafe how your medical assistant, Dealatul,
tracked down a man sick with rabies, and how you were
almost sick the entire day remembering the days when
Braniste was haunted by rabies. I knew that Kalagherovich was arrested during the rabid dog time in Braniste. That event—I mean the rabies—left such an impression on you that, after all these years, the news of
someone bitten by a rabid dog made you break down. It's
therefore logical that those days should have remained
clearly imprinted in your mind, and after all you've told
me up to now, that is indeed the case. In general, the most
powerful emotions are the painful ones, the feelings of
frustration. My mom told me that when she was pregnant
with Victoria she had a kind of dull pain in her back, and a
chaotic weariness came over her, chaotically, and the
waiting for her time of pain didn't frighten her; those

annoying little pains lingered in her mind, overpowering the true pain of her labor to come. They were, however, somehow useless; the final pain would bring a new life into the world. But these others embittered her days, and kept her from sleeping at night. It was a heavy burden to carry, and maybe this was one of the reasons why, at the beginning, she didn't even care about Victoria. Somehow, in her subconscious, she began, not refusing anymore to have her, but even more horrible, she wanted to have her no matter how, just to put an end to the torture once and for all. But I have an even better example to give you, about how man keeps pain most vividly inside him, about how the feeling of being menaced by danger can't be easily erased. For it remains, in any case, primordial. Here is the example: mama also told me that when my dad found out about her pregnancy (with Victoria) and was very happy, waiting like crazy to have a little girl, his happiness after a time seemed to fade, or go into hiding inside of him, and in its place appeared another emotion that made him jump at every noise, and when on the road, it made him always knit his eyebrows in watchfulness: he had begun to be afraid of rabid dogs. That they might by some chance bite mama. And I think that an expert in measuring the intensity of emotions would have found that the fear of the rabies ultravirus was predominant in my dad then, and not the hoping for Victoria. I would add that there was, in the case of both my mom and my dad, an ultra-emotion that they didn't want to acknowledge or that they didn't feel to be that horrible: it was called Kalagherovich, to name it after the name of its victim, since we don't know who the guilty person is. What was more important than her chaotic pains—but made them even worse—more important than the miniscule agent whose size was something between 140–240 microns, was Kalagherovich. So, think about Kalagherovich, Nicanor. Did you ever see him? Did you know him?"

"No."

4

—I didn't know him, Tica, but I had heard of him. I'll
try to recall when I heard his name for the first time. No, I
can't remember exactly. I did know your father, or at least
I saw him many times. He used to come to Braniste with
Moses, the Patirlagele school principal. They came often.
To take a census of people, sheep, horses, and, I think, of
dogs too. Possibly. I forgot to mention that on the day I
went to the clinic after Danila—and he said that Florentine was blind—Moses' buggy was pulled up in the shade
in front of Cowskinner's house. That was before 1950.

The principal and your father were eating green walnut
preserves on the porch of the clinic, and Florentine had
gotten them some cold water from Cowskinner's American well. Danila didn't know them, and when he spotted
them, he got livid.

"Did you come to make an inspection?" he asked
them.

"No."

"Did you come for the health service?"

"No."

"From the center, in Bucharest? From the Party?"

Moses answered, smiling: "No, no, no . . ." Then he
went on to explain: "We're from Patirlagele; I came on
other business and we stopped by to see Miss
Firulescu . . ."

"Ah!" went Danila. "You stopped at the clinic to eat
some preserves, since there isn't even a cafe here . . ."

"Are we disturbing you, Doctor?"

"Not at all. It's only that preserves may not be good for
you so early in the morning," said Danila, and he went
into his office.

He hadn't gotten livid from thinking that those two were inspectors, as I had supposed; he was bothered by their intimacy with Miss Firulescu. And he couldn't master his jealousy. Moses noticed that about him too, since he said to Florentine:

"I have the impression that the young man wants to kick us out of here."

"The young man might well kick us out of his office, but here you're on the porch of the house, and as you well know, the house belongs to Cowskinner, and the clinic has only a few rented rooms," she spoke without lowering her voice, and there was no way Danila couldn't have heard her through the door that separated him from them.

And the last words, in any case, he did hear; he appeared in the doorway, dressed in his doctor's smock, paler than before.

"Wouldn't you like some preserves?" Florentine asked him.

"I'd like you to call those men of yours, the dog-catchers; I need them."

"They'll be here quick as a wink," she laughed, and she called Cowskinner and whispered something to him.

The men gathered together during the time Miss Florentine was preparing black coffee for her guests from Patirlagele. Danila strolled through the pen, now empty, through Cowskinner's backyard, out onto the road, with his hands behind his back, pale and impatient. And I, with my stilts, next to the huge mulberry tree in Cowskinner's little garden, among the ferns, was eating black mulberries.

"Doctor Danila wants to tell us something."

"Let's hear it," said Longbarrel.

"This morning when I came to the clinic, near your house, Prince, I saw a dog."

"Yes, so what?" Big Prince didn't understand.

"He was looking at the ground and wanted to get through the fence, he couldn't see, he knocked against the fenceposts and didn't even see them. And when I shouted at him he didn't hear me."

"He didn't know you."

"He was foaming at the mouth."

"So what?"

"He was turning round and round, and started chasing his tail. He wasn't good for anything anymore, he didn't even have enough strength to bite or bark . . . Don't you understand? He was rabid!"

The men laughed.

"That's a good one," said Pecker. "You mean that he was overcome with rabies?" And once again they all laughed.

"What is it that you want us to do?"

"This time it really is a question of rabies," said the doctor, frightened by their laughter.

"Weren't you the one who stopped us from catching dogs, because it was all just a bogeyman and because Milksop's daughter died of her lungs, and who only wanted to push us to have the nerve to catch *his* shaggy dog . . . ?"

"We don't snap at that bait anymore," laughed Longbarrel.

"But now it's true!" shouted Danila, as if he'd gone out of his mind, and instead of making them listen to him, his tone made them laugh all the harder, and Florentine laughed too.

The men had gotten bored with hunting dogs in the village and saying afterwards that they weren't sick. And even if it was a question of a real danger now, their boredom was so great and their disbelief so complete that all they could do was laugh . . . "We're eating preserves and people are being threatened with an epidemic . . ."

"Excuse me, but we thought you were jealous," Moses spoke.

"Of what?" answered Danila still bristling.

"You can go," Miss Florentine told the men. And their

brisk steps around the table, where the plates with preserves were laid out, and her icy look said clearly that she would have been much happier if Danila had been angry because of the guests being there. It was the dog he spoke of that made the doctor livid, not jealousy, not the glasses of cold water brought by her with a smile.

"You can leave," she repeated, and the men would have left if Moses hadn't intervened.

"Don't make them leave, Miss Florentine; actually, even if it's not all the dogs that are sick, but only one of them, they all deserve to be killed." Then Moses went over to the doctor and put his hand on his shoulder in a friendly sort of way: "You've got to try to understand them, and Miss Florentine too; they've gotten tired out . . . right Horia?" But Horia Dunarintzu didn't answer, and Moses went on: "They've gotten tired out from having to be always concerned about the lives of other people . . . and they've gotten bored with tramping around to catch dogs and kill them . . . And with telling their fellow villagers the same words: Be careful, be careful! They have their own problems . . . Right, Horia? It's ridiculous to feel that you've been transformed into a word mill . . . Everybody wants to be himself, not what somebody else wants him to be, right Horia? So that . . . Miss Florentine, they should listen to him . . . He's a doctor. The disease has to be nipped in the bud, right, Horia?"

"Okay," agreed Miss Firulescu. "Go ahead and get them . . . yes . . . ," and the men left, obedient and somehow convinced. And after a few moments, when they had disappeared around the first corner and you could hear their voices following a dog, she asked Danila, smiling: "Let's suppose you were right, although you weren't, but let's just suppose . . . Yes, but why do you take your role so damn seriously, as if everything depended on you? . . . Let things take their course by themselves. Why don't you just wait, why are you sticking your nose in this?"

"Wait for what, Miss?" asked Danila, all pale, and he

looked at the coffee cups in which Moses had begun to tell fortunes.

"Oh," she laughed, "wait for what? Destiny, if you please! I can hardly wait for the moment when destiny will intervene and solve everything unspeakably stupidly!" Everybody laughed, and even the doctor's eyes got softer. "Hey, doctor," Miss Florentine urged him, "go get a jug of cold water . . . It's such an idyllic morning that it's a shame to refuse preserves that give all this wonderful charm . . ."

And Danila brought a jug of water from Cowskinner's American well and accepted some green walnut preserves.

The amateur dogcatchers came back not long after with some ten dogs, and Florentine went into the pen with the syringe and the phials of poison, and the curs, almost strangled by the chains, died like blisters that drain out through the prick of the needle that made them. The sun was shining on their soft fur and reflected brightly from their lustrous, white or russet hair. The doctor went into his office, fleeing so as not to see the death that he had wanted.

"He wants to eradicate the virus but feels sorry for a few dogs; you can't have it both ways," said Moses.

And Horia Dunarintzu looked him right in the eye and said:

"Yes, yes, I understand . . ."

"It's simple," said Moses.

"Yes, it's very simple . . . I understand you, Moses."

"Why understand me?" the principal wondered.

"I understand why you brought me here in your buggy, why you kept me here on the porch the last time too, when Miss Florentine injected dogs . . . Back then I didn't understand anything . . ."

"I don't get what you're trying to say."

Moses lit a cigarette, and the way he moved the lighted match through the air and put it out, crushing it in his coffee cup, made me recall the day when I myself had seen the killing of the dogs, and when I had seen those two on the porch of Cowskinner's house, and I hadn't paid any attention to them; the flame of the match reminded me of a gesture back then, and that gesture superimposed itself exactly on the one I was seeing now. Therefore Moses' thoughts from back then should be superimposed exactly on what he was thinking now. Horia Dunarintzu was right, they had been here before. He said:

"I understand, Moses, why you brought me here today too, because you supposed that Miss Firulescu would be injecting dogs again . . ."

"It's her job, it's normal for her to take steps . . ."

"Yes, but you brought me here not, perhaps, to see her, but to see how easy it is to die from a gram of poison, within a few moments . . . A simple prick of a needle and that's it . . ."

"You're crazy," laughed Moses, "you got drunk on cold water."

"If only that were so . . . You wanted to show me this as a possibility . . . No, no, Kalagherovich isn't what you think . . ."

"But I don't think anything, I only asked you what you know about him . . ."

"Might he perish like that from an injection?"

"Nonsense, who has any reason to kill Kalagherovich? If he's guilty, he'll pay. Why do you see the dark side of everything?"

"Then it's about me? If I don't talk!"

"Come on, let's go, you're rambling. You don't need to worry, you don't have any reason to, you're honest."

"That's just why I'm afraid," said Horia Dunarintzu. And he watched Moses who was holding another lighted match in the air, attentive; for he had a feeling that there was someone in back of him. And there was: Danila was next to the porch, in the grape vines planted by Cowskinner; he had come out of the clinic through the door leading to the kitchen and had come silently, perhaps to talk to the dogcatchers; and he stayed there, mute, listening to the discussion between Florentine's two guests, whom he still didn't have any reason to like. Sensing him more than seeing him there, Moses put out the match in the air and laughed to make it seem like a joke that they had chatted about before. But Danila, looking pale, asked them:

"Who is Kalagherovich?"

5

"Ha, ha," Moses forced a laugh also at Pecker's daughter's wedding when Danila asked him the same question, and like the first time, at the clinic, he gestured with his right hand toward the nurse and told him to ask her. And when Danila asked her, deafened by the trumpets and the drums of the musicians, as he had been deafened in the clinic by the hoots of the dogcatchers and the blows of their clubs against the fence, she shrugged her shoulders, the same as the first time, and only answered with another question:

"Who is Kalagherovich?"

"That's what I'm asking you," Danila took up the discussion again in the same words as before.

And she, drinking a glass of wine and looking at him over his head it seemed, without seeing him, or wanting not to see him, answered him lazily with his own reply: "That's what I'm asking you."

Horia Dunarintzu was at the wedding too; or rather, he happened to come to the wedding by chance, brought, perhaps not by chance, by Moses in his buggy. I say by chance because Horia Dunarintzu didn't know it was Pecker's daughter's wedding that day, he thought it was the next Saturday, and the proof was that he was wearing everyday pants made from other military pants, dyed a nut-shell brown. Moses had even changed his shirt, which Horia Dunarintzu didn't notice until he saw him joining in the hora, called in by Galatioan. That was, apparently, Dunarintzu's third surprise, after he had seen the wedding and the shirt, and he smiled and also joined in the hora, he too called in by Galatioan, and he said to Moses:

"You knew."

"What did I know?"

Here they interrupted their discussion, I mean they were interrupted by Danila with his: "Who is Kalagherovich?" The musicians were in the middle of Pecker's front yard, under the mulberry tree, and the hora was turning around them, and I, on stilts, next to the mulberry, saw the whole wedding in all its details. Nobody looked up to see me, nobody was interested in seeing a crazy kid whom they could see on stilts the whole day long. They had gotten used to me, and I think that they had gotten used to my craziness. I hadn't gotten used to them, although I knew them; I always heard them talking or laughing in a different way, and they were always different to me, as if they were born again every day. Not all of them, it's true. Not Danila. He always walked the same line: "Who is Kalagherovich?" And since the nurse answered him with his own question: "Who is Kalagherovich?"—that name stuck in my mind like a game where one person asks and the other answers, not only with the same words, but in the same tone of voice. At this Danila got angry for nothing; she wasn't making fun of him. I would have sworn then and would swear now too: she wasn't mocking him to make fun of him; she was mocking him to stir him up. So that he would ask her again. So that they would have something to talk about. I mean, it was clear: she didn't have any words for him except his words to her, and she didn't want to change them. Danila was, however, deaf and blind; he was the blind one, not she.

"Dammit," he said.

"Dammit," she said too.

Later I realized that he hadn't yet noticed that Florentine had fallen in love with him and was teasing him. He wanted to know who the man was he had heard about by accident at the clinic, the one who might be going to die, and she had no way of knowing that name, and thought it was a name he made up as a joke for the two of them: Kalagherovich sounded like a funny word. And since Florentine Firulescu didn't answer him as he would have liked, he became more and more convinced that this man had been her lover, or must be now. And he pronounced the name with a bitter hatred that made her burst out laughing. Between two horas I heard Galatioan, as he was lighting his cigarette with a lighter in the form of a pistol, ask the principal from Patirlagele:

"How does this guy know about Kalagherovich?"

Moses' eyes popped wide open, as if he were surprised, which meant that he didn't like the idea of Galatioan finding out that Danila had heard the name from him. And now it had become something more than a joke to me: Kalagherovich existed. And I too started dying of curiosity to find out who he was. Cowskinner came up next to those two and spoke to them in whispers, pointing to the russet dog on the road; he had come to the wedding too, attracted by the smell of food and the noise, and his mouth seemed to drop open. At first Galatioan didn't understand what Cowskinner wanted and what he was pointing out to him.

"It's yours," said Cowskinner.

"What's mine?" bristled Galatioan, somehow afraid that he might have something of his.

"Your dog," repeated Cowskinner, throwing over the fence a chunk of bread that he had taken on purpose from the table.

"He's not mine," Galatioan cut short his enthusiasm.

"He's your parents' dog, which means that he's . . ."

"I don't have anything of my own," Galtioan told him firmly.

And I didn't understand until much later why this man disowned even an ordinary dog, and why he needed to show that he wouldn't be tied to anything of his own. I supposed then that he refused to own up to the mutt so as to end a discussion that made him feel uncomfortable because of Cowskinner's grovelling that he didn't need and that annoyed him, just as it made me sick too, although to me it was also funny in a way. But Galatioan went further: he swore at the dog, and then Cowskinner didn't dare throw bread to the shaggy dog anymore so as not to anger the master who had broken off with the mutt, and he stayed there with the unthrown bread in his hand, not knowing whether to put it back on the table, or to stuff it into his pack, so he wouldn't annoy still more the man who had turned his back on the road, scowling. Moses understood that moment of hesitation, being more open-minded and more courageous. You don't know what to do at a particular moment, and you can lose everything, just as Cowskinner lost all of Galatioan's interest and regard.

"A dog is a dog," said Moses, and I didn't understand why he said that, or why he gestured to Cowskinner to leave them alone.

"Kalagherovich is a dog," said Galatioan to Moses, once alone.

Well, of course, I smiled to myself, having found out who Kalagherovich was, and wanting to tell Danila as soon as possible: it was the russet dog who was called that! In other words, it was him they were talking about at the clinic, not about a man but about Galatioan's parents' dog. It was a name only a few people knew, or a nickname, it didn't matter anymore. The shaggy russet dog, given the fearfulness of the vilage people, was not to die, so that his master wouldn't be angered when, as a matter of fact, the master, or even if not the true master but the son of the master, the one they feared, didn't give a damn about the fate of the mutt. He didn't care—which was very serious, and meant that a double danger hung over them: he could get angry if they touched the dog, or if they didn't. Then Moses, with his very keen instincts, did something unbelievable: he picked up a rock from the ground and threw it at the russet dog, hitting him squarely and making him run for it, barking. The whole wedding stopped for a moment, shaken by dread, which proved that Cowskinner wasn't the only one who had his eyes on the dog: everybody, instead of partying, had one eye on

Galatioan and one on the dog. Moses' incredible courage made them grow pale. And since they were already pale from the dust or from drink, that whiteness, the color of dread, made them turn to chalk: that is, for a moment they appeared to be made of chalk, not of flesh and bone, but of stone, burned and then extinguished. And maybe it was from there that came the respect or fear or whatever you might call the obedience that everybody showed Moses later on, for many years. Galatioan was on his side, if he didn't say anything when Moses threw the rock; on the contrary, he took him by the shoulders and they sat down together at the table. He was on his side, or maybe even more terrifying, there was someone bigger than Galatioan who was on his side, whom even Galatioan was afraid of. I don't know if that was it or not, and it doesn't even matter, since at that moment Moses was only acting on his own instincts. He had seen a terrible truth: Galatioan didn't want to admit that he had anything, and thus that he was attached to anything of his own. Anyone who is attached to anything of his own, even a trifle, might become attached to more in the future; and then he would be lost. To put it more clearly: Galatioan wanted to see everything swept away, even if it meant sweeping away things that were his own too.

"Doctor," he said to Danila, "why do you allow stray dogs to wander through the village?"

"What dogs?"

"Dogs," said Galatioan.

"Fantastic," laughed Danila.

"What's so fantastic, doctor?"

"You're fantastic! You're blaming me for something that's your fault. That dog is yours, not mine, and nobody wants to catch him!"

"I like it that you're speaking openly."

"Why shouldn't I?"

"Right," said Galatioan. "The dog isn't mine, and even if he were, now that cases of rabies have been reported, it's clear that . . . It's clear, isn't it?"

"The interests of the community are more important than anything else," said Moses.

"You make me laugh," laughed Danila.

"Why?"

"Because you say dumb things."

"Why?"

"Because you say dumb things, man! Whoever said it wasn't in everyone's interest, whoever said otherwise? Or is it in my interest, or in yours?"

"What I wanted to say is that . . ."

And here Moses got infuriated at the doctor for saying things that could tarnish the courage he had demonstrated earlier.

"You, doctor, are you trying to make yourself look good by making fun of me?"

"How did I make fun of you?" Danila didn't understand.

"You should take care of your own job," Moses' voice rose, "that's what you're paid for, not for talking!"

"But I don't understand you, what am I to blame for?"

"I'm not going to discuss it anymore," said Moses.

"Come on, let it go, we're at a wedding," Galatioan patted Moses on the shoulder.

And that was the principal's second victory of the day, and Danila's first defeat. Horia Dunarintzu had a bitter smile, but didn't seem to notice what was going on right before his eyes. You, Tica, tell me that back then your father was still a believer; what he was a believer in, you never said. The main thing is that you're right, he was a believer, he didn't look disappointed or frightened. I remember that before, in the hora, he danced next to the bride and said something to the bridegroom that made everybody burst out laughing. Then I saw him drinking with Lereu at one end of the table, and from their discussion I learned that he had been to war with one of the gypsy's brothers who had never returned home.

"Maybe he's a prisoner . . ."

"No he's not," said Lereu.

"Maybe he was missing in action and will come back . . ."

"He won't come back, he's dead . . ."

"I don't believe it," said Dunarintzu.

"Why don't you believe it? Didn't I tell you that I got a paper saying that he died?"

"I don't believe any papers."

"You, sir, are drunk; it was written on a paper!"

"He's not dead, man!"

Dunarintzu was almost shouting, but not too many people could hear him because of the din and the musicians. You say that back then he didn't believe in death yet, which is possible. He didn't believe in it or accept it; he was like a child who doesn't know what death is (although he had seen it in the war), or like an animal who is ignorant of it. It's true, he wouldn't listen to Lereu at all, and kept on saying stubbornly: no, no! Lereu remembered their discussion years later and told that it ended with Dunarintzu saying:

"Yeah, maybe."

He had accepted something, however had placed that "something" under a question mark. Lereu said:

"He died, man, why don't you allow him to die? He died for his country."

"Pardon me?" replied Dunarintzu, as if until then he hadn't been present at the discussion.

"He died for his country, he was lucky enough to die for his country."

"Yeah, maybe . . ."

"Other people didn't have even that much luck," said Lereu.

"Yeah, maybe . . ."

And then, right after those words, Pecker, who was drunk, started to bark. He had gotten smashed at the beginning of the wedding, and had walked around the front yard dragging his feet. He started to bark in time with his

steps. Cowskinner, drunk as a sailor, sang to the godfather nasally:

Oh, godfather dear, to hell with you
Do you know who you're marrying me to?
The ugliest girl we have in town,
A lazy fence prop who lets anyone under her gown.

The godfather laughed and covered his mouth with his
hand, so the bride wouldn't hear him and get angry. But
the bride went into the house with the bridegroom and
didn't have time to get angry.

"Bow-wow-wow," barked Pecker at the godfather, rub-
bing his forehead and his neck with his hands and screwing up his face as if overcome by great pain.

Then he jumped at the godfather and bit the collar of
his jacket and everybody started to reel with laughter.
The godfather was sweating and laughing, and didn't get
at all mad when Pecker tore his right sleeve with his
teeth, from the shoulder on down, so that you could see
the shirt underneath that was a different color on the
sleeves than on the front and the collar. And the whole
wedding melted in laughter when Pecker left him with
almost no jacket at all; the godfather had a short-sleeve
shirt on and it was patched under the arms. Cowskinner
shouted:

"You go to hell, you're doing it on purpose."

And he beat his fist on the table and didn't laugh anymore, and shouted at the others not to laugh anymore
either. According to him, the father and the godfather had
planned it all, to entertain everybody, to make the guests
feel happy so they would leave more money on the table.
And even when Pecker knocked the godfather down under the chairs, getting him all covered with dirt, and with
the wine and food that had fallen down, Cowskinner still
didn't stop yelling; on the contrary, he even started sobbing because no one was listening to him. Everybody
rocked with wild laughter still more when Pecker grabbed

the tablecloth with his teeth and turned over all the
plates and the bread onto the ground, and they didn't
calm down any, even when he tried to bite the godmother
on the nose. Only when his legs gave out and he fell on
his back, and tossed about like somebody in a fit of falling
sickness did people start to calm down a little, but not so
much from being horrified at what they saw as from hearing Cowskinner's voice:

"He's gone mad! He's gone mad!"

Cowskinner, however, was the most horrified; that is,
he had understood; Pecker hadn't planned anything with
the godfather, no, Pecker had gone mad. "Good Lord
above," Cowskinner bowed in prayer, weeping, "I never
before saw with my own eyes a man lose his mind, Lord,
this one has gone mad, mad."

People weren't roaring with laughter at Pecker anymore; but you could hear some of them hiccoughing from
too much laughing. They couldn't bring themselves to
believe what Cowskinner believed, just as they hadn't
believed him the first time when he yelled: "You're doing
it on purpose!" They forgot about Pecker and gathered
around Cowskinner, and some of them even took him by
the arm and led him out into the backyard and poured a
bucket of water over his head as a joke, to bring him back
to his senses.

"He's gone mad!" yelled Cowskinner even after that.

"Why would he go crazy right at his own daughter's
wedding, Cowskinner?"

"Out of joy, out of joy, he lost his mind out of joy,"
shouted Cowskinner, even when they poured the third
bucket of water over him.

And to have even wilder fun, they acted like Pecker: I
mean, they started barking. I don't know who had the
idea first of barking at Cowskinner to drive him out of his
mind too, and to see what he would say when he saw
someone else barking and going crazy, the way he believed you could go mad from joy—this time from the joy
that comes from laughter and drink, since not any of

them was marrying off a daughter and busting their buttons from becoming parents-in-law. Everybody was coming out of the shelter made of posts stuck in the ground with a wooden frame between them, and with rugs spread out on the thick frame serving as walls so that neither the wind nor rain would blow inside through them, and the whole covered over with rugs and with cardboard coated with tar; everybody, then, was coming out of the shelter that had been constructed in a single day in the front yard, and where the food was being served—so as to have room for all the guests, because there wouldn't have been enough space in the house, and it would have been too hot in the rooms—and as they were coming out, they saw some people barking in the yard and they all went wild and started yapping too, having noticed that Cowskinner was dripping wet and yelling like a madman: "He's gone mad! He's gone mad!" The musicians were eating under the mulberry tree, happy that no one was paying any attention to them, when in through the open door, from the road, came Margherita, nicknamed Iron Ass, or The Stork, since every year a stork would fly over her and bring her a child, although no one knew where it brought it from or whose it was, and she didn't know either, not because she didn't care, like those who love going to bed don't care, but because she was looney and didn't know who she went to bed with or when. Margherita was carrying her latest born in her arms, and she was rocking it and singing to it to quiet it, but the child was quiet and good. Lereu, when he saw her, ran up to her and took her by the hand, gypsy though he was, and she a Romanian woman, and although it wasn't proper, or maybe it was just considered not proper for an ugly gypsy, as they say, to touch one of ours—he touched her, I mean, he took her by the arm and led her out the door before the owners of the house, or the others at the wedding who were tipsy from *tzuica*, had a chance to see her. She had no reason to be at the wedding; everybody said she brought bad luck and kept her at as much of a distance as possible, and what's

more, believed that she was a witch, when she was just a
poor, crazy woman, only good for humping in the dark at
her house, or during the day in the woods, or the hay-
fields, or the cornfields where she could meet up with
anyone roaming around. She sat down on the ground,
without even having glanced at him, she was so used to
the idea that, when you come down to it, all men are just
alike in spite of their age, or how tall or short they are, so
that they have only one idea in mind, which was very
easy to carry out. That is to say, they were cheap, as Lereu
said she might think, although she didn't have any way of
saying it in plain words, or of putting it all together since
she was totally mindless. Maybe Lereu was right after all:
she didn't judge things with her mind, her judgment came
from other parts of her, from all those other parts that
kept her alive without a mind, and kept her eating, and
going, and working, and even giving birth to girls and
boys; her judgment came from where, even in animals,
the drive to live comes, and even the ability to see the
world and figure out, ultimately, what's what, just as animals can tell hot from cold. Lereu cared about Margherita
very much, and many people were sure that he had gotten
under her skirts, and even I wouldn't have been able to
say yes or no, and therefore I wouldn't state my opinion
and take sides, either with those who saw in the gypsy's
self-indulgence with a Romanian woman ten years
younger than him a sin that deserved—according to
them, I don't know why—the edge of a spade in the head,
or with those who found it funny to think of such a relationship between bloods of different colors (in gypsies,
said these people, the blood is darker, for skin color comes
from the blood)—so, I wouldn't take sides, not out of fear
of saying yes or no, but because saying yes was as dumb as
saying no. And Lereu wasn't attached to Margherita
through going to bed with her, because in that way he
could have been attached to another woman, or still another. He cared about her for another reason that was
much more serious: namely, that if he had a great deal of

respect for himself, and said he had his reasons for it—since he was the living proof that you can live in this world without having anything at all—for Margherita he had a thousand times more reasons for respect; she showed through her life that one can live in this world even without a mind.

Sometimes he even swore at her out of envy, and told me (only me, a child, and maybe a crazy one too, who wouldn't sell him out to anybody) that she was better off like that: "Lazy whore likes to live like that, she doesn't care!" When he led her out of Pecker's yard, I took off after him and caught up with him right next to the gate posts on the road. They were arguing.

"Where are you going with that sick child, why didn't you leave him at home?"

He was speaking to the wind, and even he knew it was dumb to talk to a mindless person about a house: his house was wherever he, or in this case she, happened to be. She looked at him with her big, blue, innocent, smiling eyes and didn't understand a thing, and kept on rocking her baby. And when Lereu reached out his hand to feel if the child still had a fever, he pulled it back as if it had gotten burnt. And he looked at me and said, once again putting his hand on the face of the one in diapers: "he's cold."

Margherita didn't hear him, or heard him only with her ears, and the words stayed only in her ears and didn't go any further, and she opened her blouse and pulled out her white breast swollen with milk, and put the nipple in the little one's mouth.

"He's dead," said Lereu, trying to get her away from the wedding, "leave him in peace, he's dead."

But she pulled the child's lip down with her thumb and pushed the nipple into his mouth, and then pressed on her breast with her hand, and I saw the flowing white milk come out of the corners of the mouth of the babe in her arms.

"Hey you, he's dead," said Lereu.

And still she didn't understand, because maybe she couldn't understand what death is, surely she didn't understand, didn't have the slightest idea what it was, and continued to nurse the dead child.

"She doesn't understand," Lereu said to me, "the idiot doesn't understand, and maybe it's better, yes it's better," he said, and took her firmly by the hand and pulled her after him toward her house.

From the backyard you could hear the barking of the wedding guests, and the song of the musicians who had been gotten up to work. Galatioan's shaggy dog appeared again, and made mouths fall open among those who had taken up the hora once more, and who were barking while dancing and making Cowskinner dance too, by force.

"What's Pecker doing?" a musician asked the bridegroom, wanting to know if he was drunk and had come back to his senses a bit, or was what Cowskinner was yelling that he was, and could thus no longer be placed in the ranks of men; and he, the drummer, wanted Pecker to be drunk, and the next day or the day after, to be a sober man once again, so that he would be able to pay them all the money agreed on for playing.

The bridegroom didn't answer until almost an hour later when he asked him again: "He's turning around in circles, as if to catch his tail, if he had a tail; he's turning 'round in circles to catch the tail he doesn't have."

"Ah!" said the drummer, then he whispered to the saxophone player:

"They didn't agree on the dowry and it's brought discord between them; he tried to make out that his father-in-law is a crazy coot who's turning in circles chasing after his tail."

At a corner of the table, the only ones left were Galatioan with Moses, and Horia Dunarintzu and Danila with Miss Florentine Firulescu. Lereu came and took them out into the front yard, having in fact called only for Danila to have a look at Pecker.

"What's the matter with him, is he sobering up?"

"No, he's not sobering up."

"Then what's the matter with him?"

"He's rabid."

"Bullshit," Danila said to him. "You seem to be cursed with being able to see only bad things and ruining every party with idiotic bits of news like this."

"It's not my fault, doctor, but Pecker was trying to bite his hands, and he would have bitten them if I hadn't tied him tightly with his back and head stuck up against a board."

"Untie him," said Danila.

"I did untie him, and I took him from the house out into the backyard; look at how he can't stay on his feet."

"He's drunk, man!"

"Could be, doctor, that the *tzuica* might have brought on the disease faster, but it would have come anyhow; look at how he's holding his head in his hands in pain!"

"Put him to bed!"

"Throw water on him, like on Cowskinner, to wake him up," said Florentine.

And some people wanted to throw water right away, but Pecker, when he saw them coming with water, tried to run away, which amused them all. Everybody, except Lereu, thought he was drunk like Cowskinner, or that Cowskinner was drunk like Pecker.

"Don't you see that he's closing his eyes, he can't stand the sun, don't you see that he can't bear the sunlight?" Lereu asked nobody in particular, probably everybody. Then he pulled down a blanket from the entrance way of the shelter that had the wedding table, and fanned Pecker with it, who protected himself from the draft and tried to run away again.

"He's running away from the draft, look how he's running away from the draft," said Lereu.

"Let's pour water on the gypsy, 'cause this one's lost his marbles from drinking too, like Cowskinner," said Big Prince.

And his brother gave Lereu a bath with a bucket of

water. But he, all wet, didn't quit; he fanned Pecker with the blanket.

"Up with the blanket, like at bullfights, like at bullfights, Lereu!" said Moses. "But watch out you don't get pricked . . ."

"Come on, let's put *him* in the blanket," Longbarrel was heard to say.

Then they shoved Lereu into the blanket by force and rolled him up into a ball, in the blanket, and started to throw him up in the air, blanket and all, like a bag of meat. And once they didn't catch him after they threw him up, and Lereu fell into the dirt and moaned violently, and was quiet as the tomb for a while, and no one had the nerve to open up the blanket to see if he had broken his neck or his back. But just at that moment of silence full of fear, they saw Danila next to Pecker, and saw his eyes, and heard him saying what, in fact, the gypsy had told them earlier, and they didn't dare even to move in that silence, or to laugh again. That silent moment stretched out, spread over the whole wedding, and grew like a swelling; and in its muteness, Lereu got up out of the dirt, brushing off the seat of his pants, black and blue only around both eyes as if he were wearing blinders—two bruises running from each ear to the base of his nose— and he went up to Pecker whom everyone had moved away from except Danila, frightened of his illness, of his teeth and fingernails, and of the air he breathed which could make them be like him in his helplessness, and in the road he had started down. The whole afternoon cooled off as if in an eclipse, and the alcohol cleared out of heads and legs, and when Danila told the whole wedding to leave for the hospital in Cimpuletz, for tests, nobody said no, and everybody got into wagons or onto bicycles or onto horses and, speechless, went out onto the road to Turnuvechi, and they had hardly reached the end of the village when they realized where they were headed and what might be waiting for them there, and weeping came upon them like an earthquake, and they went out of the

village, wailing and hiccoughing with terror, and when
they passed by the cemetery, night seemed to have very
nearly entered into them, and they mourned in each
other's arms, each mourning the death of the other, and
mourning their own death too, and their dead body of
tomorrow. As for Pecker, they put him in a big chicken
coop made out of wooden slats, with his hands and feet
tied, and he was forgotten by everybody, for no one had
time anymore to think about anybody else. They felt
around on their hands and feet, and had also pulled off
their shirts, overblouses and pants—to see if they were
bitten somewhere without their knowing it, while they
were asleep or who knows when, by the teeth of a dog, or
by who knows what rabid mouth, and although they
didn't find any fresh wounds, old scars they did find, and
since no one knew how Pecker got rabies, one could as-
sume that rabies could have been inside of each of them
for a long time and show signs of itself at any moment.
Galatioan's shaggy dog, following along after the convoy,
had appeared, as was his custom, there where people
were, and looking at the dog's eyes as he was watching
them cry, the people pulled themselves together sullenly
and didn't cry anymore, and then you could hear instead,
the creaking of the wagons; and the anxiety spread to
Moses' buggy, where Horia Dunarintzu and Galatioan
had found room—Galatioan with his face pale too from a
terror that came from beyond the human, from a threat
that can't be opposed because it's invisible and blind and
could put him, like anybody else, where Pecker was. He
saw the chubby dog following them like a curse, russet
colored and shaggy and saucy, and he understood the suspense in the stillness of the voices that weren't getting
hoarse from so much silence, and I don't know what else
he understood or what else he thought when he put his
hand in the back pocket of his black pants and pulled out
a much bigger lighter than the first one, just as shiny and
in the shape of a pistol, and I thought he was going to light
a cigarette, but noticed only when I heard a deafening

bang that he didn't have a cigarette in his mouth. The russet dog didn't even yelp, he fell, hit right in the forehead, or right in the heart, I don't know which; what I do know is that he died like a flea, taken to another world with one squeeze, within half a moment, without writhing, or without even having the time to be tortured, or to be surprised. He remained in the wagon tracks, in the horse manure, but it seemed to me that Galatioan's quick decision was based on a bigger decision that he had been keeping inside him for a long time, otherwise he wouldn't have been so absolutely without any trace of a good or bad expression on his face when he fired. Because even among the people who wanted the russet dog finished off, you could see that some of them were upset when faced with the dog who fell, struck down, and maybe not quilty . . . but even if guilty of having some disease, he still fell, not quilty, and for some people that wasn't anything to be happy about. Galatioan had also proved, in front of everyone, what he had told Cowskinner several hours before, that the russet dog wasn't his. Okay, he threw off something that still, everyone knew was his, to show them all that he could do without anything, if he wanted; okay, I understood that, and also how in firing a shot, he wanted to show that he, himself, had what others didn't have, and how he was protected by the shining lighter, which wasn't a lighter like the white pistol he lit his cigarette with when he smoked; I understood his pride in having what other people didn't possess, and in being able to do what was forbidden to others, both in law and in fact; I understood, okay. But it seemed to me, from the haste with which he aimed and fired, that I saw the same thing, in a different form, but still the same thing that I had found in the wailing of the other people: that the road to Cimpuletz they had to go on was a road with no future, it could for any one of them end anywhere, even three steps away; because no one could be sure he hadn't caught rabies and wouldn't, from one moment to the next, start barking; and barking meant not only becoming an animal, losing all one's human qualities inside the outer shell of a man; no, in falling from the ranks of the human you didn't just fall into the ranks of the animal, you fell straight into death. When you start to bark, you start to die. That was the terror that not even Galatioan could get around, even if he hadn't wept in Moses' buggy. The pistol shot was like a shout of horror. And note that he who said that nothing was his, not even his own folks who didn't come to the wedding, nor his own belongings, he was just like everybody else on the road going to Cimpuletz, and therefore wasn't the way he said he was, except on the outside. Inside him glimmered the fear of rabies, just as it glimmered in me, and in Lereu, and in all of us who had to go to Cimpuletz on a road with no future, forced to live in a time and in a life with no future. But not all places are called Cimpuletz. That you can see on any map.

6

The dog remained where he had fallen, and the next day
the stench got into him, and the flies swarmed all over
him, sticky things that they are, and especially the great
big green ones crowded around to suck out the dead sap
from him; the red blood around his forehead turned
yellow, like a crown, where death had entered into him.
Lereu pulled him by a foot into a ditch and turned over an
edge of its sandy soil onto him, burying him with the
worms that had invaded him, and with the greedy flies
that didn't want to part company from so rich a prey. In
Cimpuletz I learned from Lereu that the russet dog was
called Pantelimon.

"What was that dog's name?"

"Pantelimon," he answered me.

And I never told him that I had thought his name was
Kalagherovich, and I didn't care anymore either about
this Kalagherovich. I even forgot about him immediately,
thinking about the people who were going in and out of
the hospital. The priest from Patirlagele happened by, the
one who hadn't come to Pecker's daughter's wedding because he wasn't invited, and he wasn't since they knew
he wouldn't come to marry the bride and groom; he didn't
perform marriages, didn't believe in marriage, and didn't
want to read from holy books while censing with burning
incense and singing the Isaiah song in order to bless a
misfortune. So that people either called other priests from
other villages to weddings, or a bride and groom didn't put
wedding crowns on their heads and started their life together as a couple without the church, which is how most
of them began, and not even recorded in the register at
Town Hall, thus without being under any law; without

laws or priests it was even cheaper, and if they couldn't get along with each other, they'd never cross a threshold together, even if they'd been chained by all the laws of the world, even if seventy-seven priests would have sung to them in front of an altar. The doctors couldn't do anything for Pecker. His daughter, the bride (who had gone to the Cimpuletz hospital dressed in her lemon blossom bridal veil, holding hands with the bridegroom and trembling that they might have the disease), recalled that a dog had bitten Pecker about six weeks before, one evening when he was coming back from wool carding.

"Forty-two days and forty-two nights have passed and there's no hope," said Sevastitza when they brought Pecker to her, after the doctors had said they couldn't do anything. "If I had cut him under the tongue at that time and had broken the spell, and if I had hung wooden charms around his neck, he would have been a human being, now he's not anymore."

But she took the spell off him anyhow, and said to bring her some hair from the dog that had bitten him and gave them some hope again that she might be able to put him back on his feet, a hope that not one of them believed in. It still could have been believed in if they had known where to find the cur; but which was that dog? And might he not have been killed by the dogcatchers or by the nurse? Surely he had been killed, and now there wasn't any hope for Pecker; what his life depended on had been injected with poison. And they didn't even know where he had been buried so they could dig him up and get some hair off his back. I mean, they knew where they had been buried, but could you ever find the dog that bit Pecker among all the other rotting ones just like him—if from the start you didn't know which one he was? It was impossible. Only the person who had been bitten could recognize the cur, but Pecker didn't even recognize people anymore. So, they kept him in that wooden coop and waited for him to die, all tied up. I saw him all the time; he didn't bark anymore (though I didn't believe he even truly barked at the wedding, but that he produced some strange, inarticulate shouts that, in the uproar and laughter that was going on then, sounded like barks), he had a sadness in his eyes, and his dizziness and his thirst made his head swim. His daughter stayed beside him, and in vain would bring a jug of water to his lips again and again; he would shake and yell, and he couldn't bear to touch water, and that was his torture, that he was dying of thirst but couldn't drink water.

And in all that turmoil, everyone looked at his own dog with disbelief, and they didn't let their clubs go out of their hands even when they crawled under the covers. Longbarrel slept with a club in his arms, frightened that dogs might come upon him in his house and bite him. His cow got rabies; her eyes were red when Danila came in to look at her.

"Her eyesight's changed," said Longbarrel.

"What do you mean her eyesight's changed, because she's got red eyes?"

"No, because she doesn't know me anymore. This cow has a different sight in her eyes, poisoned, different, and it doesn't let her recognize me, her master, anymore."

"What should we do with her?" asked Danila.

"Meaning?"

"That she's rabid."

"Ah, to be sure. I'm sure of it myself, but it's good to hear it officially too."

"If I tell you no, what will you do with her?"

"I don't know, because I never had a cow run away from home before, and bite and howl."

"Miss Firulescu hasn't been by here?"

"I didn't call her. Should I call her too?"

"Call her, but where? Because I don't know where she is."

"Maybe she was called to another cow."

"Did you see a certain Kalagherovich going into her house?"

"When?"

"Now, or before."

"Not anyone, not by that name or any other. I guarded all her nights, I mean, I didn't exactly guard them, because no one paid me, I only saw them."

"How did you see her nights?"

"To put it better, her mornings; nobody went out of her house."

"Ah," said Danila.

"What does that 'Ah' mean?"

"Nothing. So, does she eat food?"

"Who?"

"The cow."

"The cow won't eat anymore. But she swallows money."

"What did you say?" laughed Danila, without believing him.

"Let's give it a try, doctor," he said, and took a fistful of change out of his pocket: old and new coins, and some from the war, and Serbian ones. He shook them in his hands like seeds, and then threw them onto a cloth next to the cow, who was tied to a mulberry tree.

"I see that she doesn't eat money."

"She doesn't eat it, she swallows it."

"I don't see that."

"Wait a bit," said Longbarrel, and he went into the shed and brought out several notebooks that he tore up and threw, in wads, onto the same cloth. The cow still didn't bend down to touch the things around her, and with a stick, Longbarrel shoved up next to her some coals he had found in the cold fireplace. "Maybe she wants some nails too," he threw some on top of the money.

And Danila didn't like it that he was having such a good time, and said: "You're laughing, huh?"

"What should I do, cry?"

"She's still not eating, we're not in a circus."

"Look at her, look at her!"

And sure enough, the cow, while grazing around the mulberry tree, walked onto the cloth too, and onto the coals that cracked sharply, and as she was swinging her head around on all sides in her delirium, her lips touched close to the nails, which she licked with her tongue, and made them disappear, along with the coins, all at once, in her wide mouth; and she also swallowed the coals, and the wads of paper, and the dirty handkerchief thrown down by Longbarrel, along with everything else he could find in his pockets: the pack of cigarettes and the box of matches.

"I could make big money on her in the marketplace," said Longbarrel, sucking his teeth with pleasure, but just then the cow grunted like a pig, seemed to neigh hoarsely, and his eyes popped out like a hanged man's, and he spat at her. "You go to hell," he shouted at her. "Get her away from me, doctor; if she breaks the chain, she'll get the fences, and the poultry, and the doors, and the beds with her horns, and she'll trample me with her hooves, and she'll swallow me too."

"You should kill her."

"I won't kill her, because if I miss and she escapes . . . I won't kill her, let the devil kill her. Give her an injection like the dogs."

"Go find Miss Firulescu."

"I'll go look for her," he said.

And he left for the village, slamming the door, happy to leave the house. He had lost the joy with which he bragged that the cow swallowed money and nails. He came back in a short while without Florentine, followed by a troop of gypsies.

"There she is," he showed them the cow, ignoring Danila, not to mention me, whom he hadn't paid any attention to before either.

"And where's it at?" asked Zapirtzan.

"What?"

"What I told you."

"On the wood pile."

"Good," said Zapirtzan, and he went over by the side of the kitchen where logs were cut for the fire, and came back with the ax over his shoulder. He struck the cow a quick blow on the head with the edge of it, and she kneeled down and seemed to squeal, and died on her knees with her head in the dirt, mingling her slobber with the coals she had crushed earlier with her hooves.

"You saw, doctor, how her voice was changed," said Longbarrel, "even her voice, not just her sight."

"Didn't you come across her?"

"You there, what do you want, *tzuica* or wine?"

"*Tzuica*," Zapirtzan answered for all the gypsies.

And while Longbarrel went down into the cellar to fill the bottle, they came into the yard with their arms full of straw. Danila went out onto the road and headed for the clinic. The gypsies made a fire, and Zapirtzan cut off the cow's head with the ax and threw it into the fire. They put cornstalks and corncobs and dry willow branches on too, and after they had set fire also to the place where the blood had flowed out, and had buried the cut-off head, they lifted the headless cow onto Zapirtzan's wagon, brought over in the meantime by his son, and left.

"What are you going to do with the meat?"

"Eat it."

"That's your business," Longbarrel washed his hands of it.

"You told us what?"

"To get rid of the cow for me!"

"We got rid of her."

"You shouldn't . . ."

"Don't worry," laughed Zapirtzan, "I threw away the head . . . rabies is in the head."

I went to tell Danila not to let them eat meat stricken by rabies, or at least to tell Lereu. I didn't find them even at Pecker's where Sevastitza was putting a copper coin on an old, closed wound of his and taking the spell off him, muttering something incomprehensible.

The bridegroom brought a young, white male dog, almost hanged to death, and said to the old woman: "Here he is"—and at that moment he hit him in the middle of the head with the edge of a hoe, and struck him again until he smashed his skull to bits. "He's rabid, he's the one," he told the bride too.

 And he put an old worn-out mat filled with straw on top of him, and from the kitchen got a piece of burning wood that was blazing at one end, and thrust it like a spear into the mat. At first, putrid smoke came out, then the straw caught fire, and the dog's white hair started to stink. They brought the coop with Pecker in it to where the smoke was, and since the straw was just about to be all burned up within a moment or two, she sprinkled it with water from the bucket to slow it down.

"You have to get a lot of smoke to him from the dog hair."

"Yes, you do," said the bridegroom, and he got into the smoke too, although he didn't think he had been bitten by anything, but it wouldn't do him any harm. Maybe that way he could strengthen his blood so that in case he happened to get bitten, he would be safe.

"If they had gotten him into the smoke at the beginning, he would have been saved for sure," said Sevastitza.

The bride wasn't going around anymore dressed up, and was wearing everyday skirts and blouses, but she was still in the wedding week and so "bride" remained her only name, and the bridegroom kept shouting at her: "bride!" She too got into the smoke from the burning hair that was smoldering in the embers, sneezing; and she, and the others were only pretending, or maybe they truly believed, not having anything else to believe in, not having any other dog to believe in, that the white one was the guilty one, and therefore was rabid, although good God, from the way the bridegroom dragged him in the noose, he only looked like a guiltless and very dumb, or very trusting, poor doggy who let himself be caught in the middle of a field. He wasn't from the village, he was from somewhere else; the bridegroom came upon him by chance in the grazing lands, he admitted that himself; but then how the hell could he swear that this was the one they were looking for? Everybody believed him, and didn't even doubt for a moment that it might be otherwise. The bride, after she had gotten herself all black from the choking smoke—they had thrown more wet straw on the dog— told Sevastitza that it seemed to her that she had been bitten by a dog too, by that one or another, she really didn't know, and didn't know when either, today, yesterday, or some other time. She even showed a scratch on her left leg that could have been from either a dog's tooth, or a scrape from a fall, or a prick from a bramble.

Sevastitza put a copper coin on her wound too, and took the spell off her, and ended up like this: "Don't forget the coin, you'll give it to me after you're cured." Then she put ashes on the wound from the hair of the white mutt, and some garlic mixed with salt.

"Cut me under the tongue too," begged the bride.

No one stopped Sevastitza (not even Florentine Firulescu who appeared at the end to see why a fire was burning in Pecker's backyard) from sharpening her razor on a wide belt, and from opening up the bride's mouth and cutting the "little dogs" under her tongue. I saw a few streaks of blood on the razor, but I didn't hear a sound from the bride's mouth; terror seemed to have taken away all her words. She believed so strongly that a dog had bitten her, and that only by cutting the evil gathered under her tongue could she be saved. Everybody seemed to have gone mad, and they were only waiting for Sevastitza to tell her what else she had to do.

"Now you can sleep in peace, I cut your 'little dogs,' my girl. I only have to put the charms on you and that's it!"

The dog burst open from so much fire that had cooked him, and the bridegroom put more straw and cornstalks and wood on him until he turned completely to ashes and disappeared—and it seemed awful to me to see something just stop being, and see how easy it can be for something to stop being anything even when it's dead, something that had been alive before, with feet, tail, head, ears and eyes. When Danila appeared also, brought by Longbarrel to meet with Florentine, he wasn't even ashes anymore; the bridegroom had swept them into the marsh next to the well where the ducks bathe.

"Look at Longbarrel there too," said Sevastitza. "How are you; say, you've still got that big lump, it's never gone away?"

"There you go, shooting off your mouth again. You lost your chance to shut up."

"Why should I shut up, huh, big lump?" She laughed and went into the house after the bride.

"What lump do you have, Longbarrel?"Danila took him by the arm.

"I don't have any lump."

"Yes he does, yes he does," laughed Sevastitza, "just pull down his underpants and you'll see what a big lump his mama made him with!"

Danila started questioning his assistant in front of everyone: "Where are you wandering off to, miss?"

"Are you talking to me?"

"To you, of course, not to me," said Lereu, who had come in through the gate, "since I'm not a miss, or maybe not even . . ."

And here he stopped. He had, perhaps, wanted to say: or maybe not even you are a "miss" anymore if you don't feel like one. He didn't say it; Danila stopped him harshly:

"You, don't stick your nose where it's not your pot that's boiling."

"Maybe," laughed Lereu.

And I think he wanted to say: maybe mine is boiling. He didn't say it; Danila jumped at him again:

"You'd better not let those people eat meat from a sick cow."

"They eat even when they know it's dead things, and still in vain."

"What do you mean, in vain?"

"Well, in vain because they still don't die. They fry it,

and they boil it, and there's no way for the evil not to get cracked away; fire rescues you from all your woes."

"Drop it . . ." Danila went on.

But he didn't know what else to tell him in order to convince him. He wasn't at all in the mood for Lereu, and so didn't find any more words for him. Only for Florentine.

"Where were you all morning?"

"In Cimpuletz."

"What do you go to Cimpuletz for every day?"

"I don't go every day, I only go on Thursdays."

"The hell Thursday, today is Friday!"

"Yes, it's Friday."

"So you were there both yesterday and today, without asking me!"

"Why should I ask you, do you ask my permission for anything?"

"But I'm your boss!"

"He, he," laughed Florentine. "My bosses are in Cimpuletz. You're not yet in charge of the clinic; I'm the only one who can sign for what goes in and out of here, so that, in fact, I'm the boss. The lady boss," she laughed in his face.

"Don't be cheeky with me! What do you go to Cimpuletz for every Thursday?"

"If you yell at me, I won't answer you. If you talk nicely, I'll tell you."

"I'm talking nicely," Danila's voice changed.

"I go to the hairdresser; the girl who does my hair works on Thursdays."

"Ha, ha," went Lereu, and I don't know if he was laughing at Danila because she went to the hairdresser and not where he feared, to who knows who—or if he laughed, meaning, whoever does your hair does a good job.

"Today is Friday, what did you go for today?"

"Yesterday the girl wasn't there, she had the day off to go to a funeral, and so I went today."

"Yes, I understand," said Danila. And you could see

that it suited him just fine to find out that she had been at the hairdresser's.

"I don't know if you understand or not, but as for seeing, you never see," Lereu stuck his nose in again. ·

"What don't I see?"

"You don't see that Miss Florentine's hair is beautifully done every Thursday."

"Well, I . . ."

"You didn't see, being busy with one thing or another, or didn't want to see, or didn't pay attention, and that's bad: not to see when a young lady makes herself more beautiful."

"Just drop it, Lereu."

"Oh no, I'm not going to drop it; for you not to see, that means you're not interested."

"In whom?"

"In Miss Firulescu, your servant, since you are after all her boss, as you said; and if you didn't care about her then, what right do you have to yell at her now? 'Cause you're yelling as if you were head over heels in love."

"Come on, come on, stop it, Lereu, don't take advantage of my friendship to make up all kinds of nonsense."

"Are you angry?"

"Of course I'm angry!"

"Then clearly you're head over heels in love; otherwise you wouldn't care about this kind of made–up nonsense."

Only those two were still there, next to the well; Miss Firulescu had gone in after Sevastitza to see what was going on in the house with Pecker and the bride.

"You do care."

"Me?"

"Well, I guess not me! What's bad is that you didn't notice that on Thursdays she goes to Cimpuletz and is absent. You thought she was absent every day, and therefore you need her all the time, and when you aren't beside her you think she's in Cimpuletz, and she keeps getting away from you. That's good. And it's not at all a bad sign."

"That she's absent?"

"No, that she's absent doesn't matter; that you feel she's absent. That's not a bad sign on your part. It means that you can feel when she's away."

"What you're trying to tell me is that I've . . . That I've what? That I've gone soft in the head, that I've fallen in love, that I've what? Because it's not clear. That I've . . ."

"That's it, I've got you. But there's a danger: she makes herself beautiful on Thursdays. Fine. The question is: for whom? Why on Thursdays?"

"Thursdays are when that girl works," said Danila.

"Bullshit! That girl works the whole week! Why Thursdays; who is she making herself beautiful for?"

"That, yeah, that is a question!"

"It is. Because it's not for you!"

"No, for sure not . . ."

"What's good is that you didn't notice that she was absent on Thursdays."

"You said before that it was bad I didn't notice!"

"No, it's good; you didn't notice that she was absent on Thursdays, therefore you felt as if she was absent the whole week, even when she was in the village and wasn't with you, and—because there is one more 'and'—not noticing that she made herself beautiful on Thursdays means that for you she's beautiful the whole week just the way she is, whether she goes to the girl to get her hair set or not. That's good. From your point of view. You're crazy about her! Now let's look at it from her point of view; who's she crazy about?"

"Who comes here on Thursdays or Fridays?" asked Danila.

"No one, usually."

"And so?"

"And so, either she does her hair for someone from somewhere else, from say Cimpuletz, or she does it for . . ."

"For whom?"

"For herself."

"What do you mean, for herself?"

"You've gotten dumb about everything, doctor! Didn't you say that she's blind in the morning and doesn't see anything except herself, or worship anything except herself?"

"I did."

"You said an even dumber thing too: that she had one altar and one god, which is herself. In other words, she worships herself, her own eyes, her own legs!"

"That's not at all dumb, it's the truth; she believes in her own flesh like in a god! She's convinced that maybe with her legs and with her neck and with her eyes, with her body . . ."

"Well, that's it! It's for herself that she makes herself beautiful! But she has something she's not happy with: her hair. She's not satisfied with it, the way it comes out when she puts it up herself, and then she goes to Cimpuletz. For her, nevertheless, for her many more men will get hot, not only Longbarrel who has no peace in the night. She knows it. And you, I see you as someone who'll fall flat on his face. And she knows that you'll fall, or might even wonder why you haven't fallen yet. Didn't you see how her eyes laughed when you yelled at her? That's a sign for her that you'd been at a loss with her, because you yelled: 'Where are you wandering off to, Miss?'"

"To hell with her, I'm not going to yell anymore, I'll show her that's not the way it is, and you'll see that it's not what you think, that you're wrong!"

"If I'm wrong, I'm not losing anything," said Lereu, and after that he was quiet—Florentine was coming out of the house.

Then there appeared in the dust of the road, as if it had sprung out of the earth, a buggy with Moses and Horia Dunarintzu, and Danila blew his nose so as to have something to do, and so as not to look like a bump on a log, and stared at his assistant's hair.

"What's new, doctor?"

"Nothing."

"Any new cases?"

"Nothing."

"No other animals got sick?" Moses then asked Florentine, seeing that, except for nothing, nothing came out of Danila's mouth.

"A cow."

"What cow?"

"Longbarrel's. It's already been killed," laughed Florentine.

"What's there to laugh about, Miss?" Danila blew his nose again and looked at the hair she kept caressing.

"Does it look bad? To you maybe."

"It's nothing to laugh about."

"No, it's not," added Moses in support of the doctor's words.

"Everybody has to be careful so as not to . . ."

"So as not to get rabid," Lereu finished the sentence.

"Right."

"Why sure. And you, doctor, who are also my boss, are the one who is supposed to, and who is paid to, protect us through measures that you take, and to cure the people of the village . . ."

"Miss, you can't cure rabies, you can only get it. There are not two varieties of it, there's only one. So, don't laugh, and don't go to Cimpuletz anymore to get your hair done when I don't have anyone else to go around the village with me to talk to every inhabitant, to get him to tie up his dogs and not let children out alone, and to keep watch over his animals . . ."

"I'll ask your permission, and if you don't give it to me, I'll take every Thursday off that suits me so that I don't go around like a frump with hair."

"I'm not telling you not to go, but to let me know, and not to laugh when you shouldn't and when you're guilty. You must understand that if you and I go around with our own personal problems and we don't tell people to protect themselves—that's the only treatment, protect yourselves everybody!—if we don't get this simple truth into their heads, or if they either won't take it in or won't listen to us, we can rest assured: they'll all die, no question about it."

"Be more optimistic, doctor," said the principal.

"Be optimistic, but not when it's a question of rabies, Principal!"

The bride appeared with wooden charms hanging around her neck like a necklace. Sevastitza followed her, and the bridegroom, and Pecker's wife, and three or four neighbors. Moses nudged the doctor, as if to ask him what he thought about the charms that were cut out of a trough, and tied by Sevastitza to Pecker's daughter's neck; Danila didn't say anything about it, good or bad.

"What have you done, old woman?"

"What I had to, Mister Principal. I did what I could." Then she looked at the bride and spoke to her as if only the two of them were there: "You have forty-two charms; every morning break one of them off the thread and throw it toward the rising sun and say: 'Go away from me! Vanish from my sight.' And after forty-two days, when you have flung them all, if you're still alive to throw the last one, then you're saved!"

"God bless you," went Pecker's wife, but Sevastitza had gone out onto the road and was turning the corner, waving her scarf.

"What do you think, doctor, about the cow?" Moses asked again, on the porch or terrace of the clinic where, a long time before, Florentine had served him preserves.

"It can't do any harm. Maybe people will be more afraid of her than of me, and that's all right with me; they'll take care of themselves. I can only fine them, the old woman can curse them, and that's something else again."

"And when she cuts them under the tongue?"

The nurse brought some *tzuica* from Cowskinner's and poured it into glasses.

"Even if I fined them, they'd still let themselves be cut under the tongue if they wanted to; and no doubt, they want to! If I stand guard over them during the day, they go to her at night. It's not the people, it's the dogs above all that you've got to keep an eye on; in them lies the danger."

"When a dog gets fat it gets rabies."

"Not exactly, Mister Principal. They should be tied up and . . ."

"And starved."

"No, Miss, they should be fed very well!"

"Everybody does that, from what little I know; they tie them up and starve them!"

"There's a belief," put in Moses, "that dogs get rabid from being tied up, especially in the spring—right Horia?"

"Yes there is."

"I don't think it's even a question of rabies," said Florentine, sitting down next to Moses.

"Quit joking, Miss."

"I'm not joking, doctor, and in any case not with you who are my boss. I'm telling you what I think: it's definitely not rabies if Baba Sevastitza smears every bite with rabbit fat and then the next day, or maybe the same day, I don't know exactly, puts a half of a lemon on it, as if on a swelling or on other poisonous bites, from snakes, and then rubs these—which are more in their heads than real bites, or are old bites that have healed—rubs them with warm oil, or rinses them with vinegar, takes the spell off the crazy people, just as she did to Pecker's daughter right in front of my eyes, with vinegar that has Margherita's name on it, the one who is alone. No, it's not, not if Sevastitza got into the act. These crazy old women who play witch have to have something to live on—just as the doctor and I live on something—and when people sense some misfortune, these old women say it's true, and they always discover something that can't be cured, a disease you can't be saved from. And here's where they're so important—in saving you! In other words, they make you healthy, and you weren't even sick; they put you back on your feet and save you from a disease you never had! If there were truly rabies in the village, Sevastitza would never get into it, and would never go around to houses with remedies, since any idiot knows (not just doctors and nurses, old women know it too) that you can't be saved from rabies except with two meters of earth covering you and separating you from the problem."

"And Pecker?" asked Moses.

"Syphilitic. Dead drunk from the wedding."

"And the tests in Cimpuletz?"

"Do you think they know what rabies is, those bums in the lab? Did the doctors in Cimpuletz ever see rabies in their life? They've read about it in books, and from what we said it is, they said the same thing, as they always do. The disease doesn't exist at all except in the madness and in the fears of the people."

"So, then you can go off to the hairdresser with your mind at ease!"

"Yes, doctor, that too. But why do you look so glum, doctor, are you sorry that, in the absence of this disease, you won't have anything to defeat? And how can you show Lereu, and Nicanor, and me, and the others that you're absolutely fantastic?"

7

"But, before I came to the village, you had already killed a pile of curs and declared rabies."

"You, who?"

"You all, the village, you yourself."

"They'll say of every dog who is dizzy from starvation, and who can't stand on his feet, and who barks with a voice that's altered by not eating, that he's afflicted with rabies. And it suited me to say yes. That way (without my having to force anyone, with them bringing dogs in on their own), we get rid of a lot of stray dogs fast, and at the same time we give people the chance to have an extra mouthful of corn pudding on the table, and not to share it with the damn curs who were of no good to them anyhow, because there wasn't any reason for them to be protected by dogs; nobody can steal anything from them, they're as poor as their own curs."

"Come on, call me names, give me a couple of slaps in the face!" said Danila with his hands up. "Call me a crook through and through. Call me a nut who invents a disease to make himself important, curse my mother too, spit on me, what are you waiting for."

"Which is to say, you can't stand to hear the truth, to hear what I believe. Then I'll shut up and let you go on with your rabies, and go on swelling up with pleasure because you're right."

"No, Miss, tell me bluntly, I like having you tell me that Pecker is syphilitic, and that I'm syphilitic too if I imagine that he's rabid, when he spends the whole day with a blanket over his head in a chicken coop, and when, in fact, the truth is that the man is making fun of me, and is pretending he's afraid of light, and is putting on an act when he foams at the mouth, as he did in Cimpuletz when he got down on his hands and knees in the laboratory corridor and howled. His daughter, the bride, is putting on an act too when she lets herself be cut under the tongue with a razor, and the whole village is in a kind of carnival; they kill their own cattle, set fire to dogs, they're having fun."

"They're not having fun, they're afraid of a stupid thing that you, pardon me, put in their heads."

"That's right, that's right, go on, call me names! I want to find out, down to the last word, what you think of me."

"I'm shutting up, and I'm going over to ask Cowskinner for some bread and cheese, since *tzuica* doesn't slide down all by itself," she said, and went out leaving the other three in silence.

I was in the mulberry tree, in the leaves, covered also by night, standing on a branch, and I had untied my stilts so as to rest my legs from their weight. And it was curious how, in her absence, Danila didn't speak ill of her and didn't try to excuse himself and say that she was raving, but laughed to himself with such pleasure that the other two thought he was laughing at her.

"She's pretty tough, isn't she?" Moses tried to find out his opinion.

"No doubt she's very, very . . ." he said, but Moses didn't have any reason to believe him. "She makes me awfully happy."

"I can believe it," laughed Moses.

Which meant that evidently he wasn't swallowing that one, but that man to man, he accepted what Danila said, although he didn't believe it, since not even Danila himself could believe that he was very happy about being insulted. Horia Dunarintzu was thinking his own thoughts, ever silent, as if absent. But Moses was mistaken in the very point he was so sure about—that Danila said he was delighted and he wasn't! It was really just the opposite: Danila was delighted that she was putting him down, saying that he was inventing a disease! Yes, yes, that way she acknowledged he had some merit: the power of discovering what isn't, even if it is just a dumb thing, but even a dumb thing can prove power, the power of the one who invented it. He was happy, he wasn't pretending; that's where Moses went wrong, thinking that he wasn't. And Moses also went wrong somewhere else: in thinking that Danila, after such an insult or such a dismissal of a disease that had somehow become his (since he was treating it), saw that disease come crashing down on him along with his belief in it, and that's where his great indignation really came from, which however he masked by saying: "She makes me awfully happy!" There were two different things at work here. It made him happy that Miss Florentine considered him cracked in the head, or fishing for compliments, so that he could hear her opinion of him and get to know her, and by getting to know her, she wouldn't be a mystery to him anymore; it was a pleasure for him, to know her. If he got rabid—one might as well use that word since it was all about rabies anyhow—to find out where she went every Thursday in Cimpuletz, and if he took every insult from her, in public, concerning him and his profession, it was all so as to get to know her thoughts, and something about her, and knowing these, to be close to her, in other words to share the same thoughts and the same paths and the same secrets with her; that's what it was! It's strange that I started to understand love at first by discovering it in other people, and only afterwards discovered it in myself, and didn't understand it anymore then, which is perhaps quite natural. In Danila it all started in rage: what does she go to Cimpuletz for?! But his anger was only a pretext (which even he couldn't have been aware of at the outset) for wanting to know her as he knew himself, or as he thought he knew himself. And Moses was wrong the second time when he thought that Danila saw his ambitions—in other words the disease—ruined. It wasn't true; he couldn't have had stupid ambitions, couldn't have wanted to keep the disease going. He was fighting to stamp it out. But you could say that this too was an ambition, as soon as Miss Firulescu told him that rabies didn't exist, and if it didn't exist, he could take his doctor's airs and go to hell with them. But no, this wasn't the case: he didn't put on the airs of a doctor, he was after all friends with Lereu and with me, I mean with people you're a friend of only when you don't put on any kind of airs. And there's this too: he believed that the disease existed. And that's the second point, or Moses' second mistake. Danila laughed as he listened to his nurse, all hot for her, but he didn't believe her for a moment. And when she came back from Cowskinner's carrying two plates with bread, cheese, onions and bacon bits, he told her, with the same smile on his face as when she left:

"Hey, did you think of any other idiocy of mine, say it, curse me!"

"I won't curse you, I'm not a cabby."

"Why do you like to be cursed, smeared, criticized, or whatever, why?"

"Because he doesn't believe me, Mister Principal," she said, with the insight of a woman. "That's why. I tell him what's really, truly true and he thinks I'm dumb."

"For God's sake, Miss! If that's the way it was, I'd never let you talk, I'd send you off to bed! But it's always good to know another person's opinion, so we don't make any more mistakes," he laughed.

"Then why are you laughing?"

"Because I'm hungry, Miss," he answered, and he was the first to start eating bread and cheese.

"It's not good to talk about unpleasant things at the table, but since I got started, I'm not going to stop. You said, doctor, that the Prince brothers' attic, storehouse, stables and barn are full of rats."

"They said it, I only observed it."

"But you observed, not that they have them, which they know, but that they're rabid. They squeaked as if stampeded, went around the yard blindly in broad daylight without even hiding, threw themselves on top of each other, jumped when they met up with a cat or a hen."

"Yes, they've got rabies. One of them might have gotten bitten by a rabid dog, or I don't know how it happened exactly."

"Exactly, it happened in a different way: they were driven mad from hunger. The Princes woke up one night without any corn in the barn (it had been taken from them), without any wheat in the storehouse because they had sold it, without any cows or pigs; and there not being animals anymore in the stable or the pigsty, nobody took food there anymore, so that the rats were left without any crumbs. And out of hunger those rats started to bite each other, kill each other, and die. Because they did die."

"If it were that simple, then not one of them would have been left. They died rabid: they're mean and bit each other, and the aggressiveness they were born with, in this case, did them in: the disease went from one to the other, carried by their teeth and their own meanness, and the circle was closed: the disease destroyed the diseased, and in killing off the diseased it went to hell too. Understand?"

"No."

"It's very simple: the evil inside of them killed them, and once the center of contagion is stamped out, the Princes don't have rats anymore. It wasn't hunger, that would have made them spread out to other places; rabies crushed them all, dead. And the place was cleared of them."

"That's a solution," said Moses.

"What?" asked Dunarintzu.

"For disease to bring death, and death to clean up the earth, and then you can start everything all over again from the beginning, according to your heart's desire."

"Why are you provoking me, Moses?"

"How am I provoking you, Horia?"

"Okay, what you're saying are Kalagherovich's words."

"You said it, just now, that they're Kalagherovich's."

"But they're not, Moses. You'd like them to be. You said these words to me before and told me to confirm them, and I didn't confirm them, and therefore you just said them again."

"And you did confirm them."

"No, I said that they were Kalagherovich's words and you interrupted me when I tried to add: words that you say are Kalagherovich's. But they're not. Although they could be, I don't see anything threatening in them."

"Then why not admit that you heard them?"

"Because I don't want to do what you want."

"The truth is more important than what I want, Horia."

"Truth also is however you want to see it, Moses."

"Truth is one thing alone."

"It is, but it can be seen from different points of view; and then it's different, because it doesn't depend on itself, but on who sees it and from where."

"Clarify, will you, Horia."

"Let's just take the words about the disease bringing death, and death cleaning up the earth . . ."

"Yes, what about them?"

"In your mouth they're fine, in Kalagherovich's you say that they're venomous."

"He was referring to us: that a disease should come and wipe us out! He also said that a disease had already come, a disease that was worse than a disease and . . ."

"Stop, stop, Moses. What do you mean by 'us'?"

"What everybody means: us, we who strive to forge a new world."

"And Kalagherovich, what does he want? Why was he in prison?"

"He was put in prison before the liberation of this country so that he could be pulled out and placed in a high position, saying that he had a good record. It's one of the enemy's methods, a red herring."

"Ah! But he could have a good record without prison, couldn't he?"

"You don't believe me?"

"Of course not."

"But this is also Galatioan's view."

"It could be even God's view and I still wouldn't believe it. Anyway, I don't believe in God."

"You don't believe in Galatioan either?"

"What's Galatioan got to do with God? I said that I don't believe anyone who tells me what you said about Kalagherovich."

"I'm not the one who said it, others did, and Kalagherovich admitted it."

"All the more so."

"Which means, Horia?"

"All the more so, meaning: the more Kalagherovich himself would admit it, the more I can't believe that he was there, you know where, as a red herring."

"You weren't there with him."

"I knew him before he went in, and I knew him after he got out, that's enough for me. You're going too far, Moses."

"What, I'm lying?"

"Not you, Kalagherovich lied in saying what you say."

"So, he's a liar who could have been even what he admits he was."

"Moses, it's very bad of Kalagherovich to lie, if by some chance it's true that he said those words and it's not all a lie from somebody who wanted to get rid of him."

"These people here don't know who we're talking about. Miss Firulescu, doctor, we're talking about . . ."

"I know," said Danila fiercely.

"We're talking about an impostor," continued Moses.

"I know," said Danila, looking at Miss Florentine's wavy hair from the hairdresser.

"You're going too far, Moses."

"But he is an impostor."

"It doesn't matter what you call him, don't you understand? It's going too far if he admits what you say; that means he couldn't take what they dished out to him."

"We don't torture anybody."

"Who's 'we,' Moses? Why the hell do you keep using this 'we'? 'We' is almost a totally impersonal person. In other words, you, X, are talking about us in our name, but how can I know what you're saying so that I can give you permission to present yourself to other people in my name, and in the name of others? I don't like the word 'we,' you can't get anybody to accept responsibility for it. Don't use it anymore, it makes me angry."

"It makes Kalagherovich angry too."

"He's right, anybody who speaks should speak in his own name and should have to answer for it in his own name."

"It's a question of social class . . ."

"A class is a collection of individuals who, if they exist and have self-respect, answer in their names and for their deeds, otherwise it's not a question of a class but of a herd. I hope you're not trying to make me believe that you confuse class and herd; that would make things worse in this case, and would be very bad if true. We must not put up with stupidity and abuses, Moses. It's going too far, if this Kalagherovich admitted what you told me. He's lying! They threatened him, they tortured him and he lied to escape. He's only human, he couldn't hold out any more and he lied, I understand him. But it was very bad for those guys to make him lie."-

"He who lies once has already lied, and will lie again."

"Go on like this and you'll end up by not having any clean person left on earth; there has never been a person who didn't lie at least once. But not every lie is evil, Moses, not every lie is criminal. It's going too far for Kalagherovich to admit and to sign a statement that he was in prison as a secret agent . . . No one goes there as an agent provocateur, and stays there when the price is having ten toenails pulled out."

"That was to make it more convincing."

"Stop it, Moses, don't say dumb things! Who would mutilate himself with the idea of getting to be someone

sometime? What assurance would he have that his muti-
lation would take him 'far'? Your reasoning is monstrous . . ."

"It's not mine."

"Then why did you make it yours? Why don't you look
at it from the outside rather than taking it on hearsay?
And you, doctor, how do you know that this man is an
impostor?"

"That's what I heard."

"Then don't say: I know. Say: I know, that's what I
heard. Or even more honestly: that's what I heard, but I
don't know."

"That's what I heard," said Danila.

"You don't know him, doctor. Kalagherovich is an honest person, and because he's too honest he's in prison now
again."

"He's in prison, since when?" Danila was startled.

"A month ago."

"Incredible!" he rubbed his hands with satisfaction and
looked at Miss Florentine's wavy hair from Cimpuletz
without hatred.

"What's he in for?" asked Florentine.

"For saying that we need a disease so that everyone can
forget everything, or so that they can all die."

"No, Moses, he didn't say that."

"Then what did he say?"

"You know very well what disease he's referring to."

"No, Horia, he was cursing the world loud and clear,
and everything that is being built anew, and it's good for a
crazy man like him to be put away so that he won't get
you confused."

"If he gets you confused, Moses, it means that he's
right."

"He's not. He wants the end of the world."

"Ho ho! Whoever put that idea in your head?"

"Maybe I didn't express myself properly. Let's say that
the world is Braniste; well, then he wants to give Braniste
the rabid rats, and the sick dogs, and all the rest, and have

them kill each other, and have the whole village perish, so that then he could come and redo everything. Only his hand would be at the helm."

"That would be a method of escaping from rabies, if there were rabies," said Florentine.

"Killing everybody, Miss?"

"Why shouldn't they die, Principal, if they're sick?" she said, and the difference in age between them decreased.

Still, Moses didn't get angry at her saying just plain "Principal" to him, and at taking the first step in that process of reducing the difference between his years and hers, which couldn't lead to any result other than that very one; except if one or both of them would throw in a word or an act that erased the years, and the reduction would take place itself, without their working at it or being aware that it was happening, the ages simply becoming equal through that word or act. Saying "Principal" to him was like using the familiar *tu* form of the verb (instead of the proper, formal "you" form). So, Moses didn't get angry, but Danila did, and said to her:

"Speak more respectfully to your elders." In that way he put her in her place and Moses exactly where he belonged in age.

"Don't take offense, Doctor, I'm not angry," said Moses, and in fact, he didn't have any reason to be angry from the standpoint that Danila feared.

"He, Kalagherovich, wanted even people living in Braniste who might be infected with rabies to die. But the question is: if there isn't any disease, as Miss Firulescu says there isn't in Braniste, then why does he want people to die?"

"If they're well, nobody will die, Moses."

"Obviously, but why does he curse them? Of course nobody is going to croak just because of his wishes, but his wishes are reactionary. Is that how you cure a disease—assuming that it is a disease—in that way? There are still some mistakes, nobody would deny it . . ."

"Up to now you've said that there aren't. You forget from one day to the next what you say, or it's not clear to you what you want to say. You're contradicting yourself, Moses. Weren't you telling us even just yesterday that it was necessary for us to 'eradicate'—that was the word you used—all the old remnants, and construct a new world? And how do you want to do the eradicating? To eradicate means to exterminate, and only diseases eradicate and exterminate, and only they don't take into account who in their path is guilty and who is not. That too is a kind of rabies: to eradicate something completely so that afterwards you'll be the only master left on the earth, in the trees, in the sky, and in the sea, who'll still remain, no matter how devastating the disease may be, and who would never get sick from human diseases."

"What are you trying to say, Horia?"

"I'm trying to say, Moses, that once again—and when I say 'once again' it means that this has already happened before—the truth has been seen from only one side. Kalagherovich was thinking of something else when he spoke about a disease."

"That we—excuse my 'we,' but I don't have another word and I haven't given it up—we get drunk on the power we have, and it would be a good thing if, once we're drunk, we'd crack each other's heads and rot away in ditches."

"No, you're beating around the bush again! In the first place, it's not a question of 'the power we have.' You don't have any power, and nobody else does either, and nobody has any right to have such power, and can't even have such power except by taking it by force from others, leaving them without protection, in other words destitute of the freedom to protect themselves. Moses, he wasn't thinking about you— about you all—which is somehow the opposite of his 'we'—he was only joking. He said it like this: we need an epidemic so that people can forget about the disaster of the war, and the misery that followed, and can forget that even now they don't have what they need in order to live, and can't have as long as the old wounds aren't healed. Do you understand what I'm saying?"

"No."

"You can't go from being very bad off to being very well off overnight, but there are some people who say that things are going very well now, and in point of fact it isn't so, and everybody sees it isn't so; they may not even be able to believe in the tomorrow that you present to them in even brighter hues when they see that you're lying now, and lying right to their faces about what they eat, and what they see, and how they dress or how they'd like to dress; it's clear that what a person can't see, in other words the future (this was after the war, several years ago), you can lie to him about even more horribly. That's why a disease is needed so that people have to protect themselves from it and break out of the spell they hoped to live under after the last war."

"Kalagherovich is just like our doctor here," said Florentine.

"Why like me?" bristled Danila.

"You've already invented rabies in Braniste."

"He's not like him," said Dunarintzu, "Kalagherovich was referring to a true disease, that truly exists and that even Moses remembers. Kalagherovich didn't invent the disease, it exists, but people don't see it or, if they do see it, don't want to see it out of fear, and so they say that it doesn't exist. It does exist, and because of it, Kalagherovich is now in prison."

"He'll have a chance to calm down there . . ."

"But isn't it sad, Moses, that he's there? He was delighted to be arrested. That's the best proof that he's right; that the disease has settled in and has turned violent, and has moved into action in the name of its germs."

"The people in Cimpuletz have come to power."

"Cimpuletz is an anonymous thing, Moses. It can only manifest itself through living beings who act in its name, but who often say only what furthers their own interests.

Kalagherovich doesn't have anything against Turnuvechi or Cimpuletz, but he does have something against people who trample on what the state says they shouldn't. Between laws and their execution, man intervenes, and if that man is Galatioan, he can change the laws through the way he carries them out; and so allow me to tell you that all this business has nothing to do with the state at all. It was said about Kalagherovich that he was kicked out of the Party because he was living with a postal employee and thus was neglecting his family; that's what was said, but we were given to understand that this was only a nice way of kicking him out, and that the story about the postal employee didn't matter. Two lies were told here: the first in absolving him in a priestly way of his affair with the employee—I say absolving him since, in fact, it absolved him from punishment he didn't deserve; that employee never existed. And second: the story that you know, Moses."

"I hold that he's guilty."

"That's the easiest thing to do. It's what Galatioan does too . . ."

"I hope these people won't tell Galatioan what you said."

"But they can go ahead and tell him, because they also know, or if they don't know everybody else knows, that Galatioan has got Kalagherovich's job now."

"I don't know," said Danila. "But Kalagherovich sounds like a very interesting person to me, to say the least."

"Good, then say the least," laughed Moses.

But it was clear that he didn't want to listen to Danila give his opinion one way or another. Nor did Dunarintzu fully grasp Moses' wish, so he continued the discussion, believing that it was good to find out what view someone from the outside might hold about Kalagherovich, someone uninvolved. As for Florentine, she was so bored that when she saw Longbarrel going into Cowskinner's backyard, she went over to him to get him to walk her home, and off she went. But before saying good-by, she told them that she was sleepy and was leaving, and she looked especially at Danila as if to ask him if he wasn't sleepy too, and if he wasn't going to leave, after all they were neighbors and could go together, but he didn't understand, or else Kalagherovich interested him more, and he didn't get up from the table, and she looked at him, furious, and after she shook hands with Moses and Horia Dunarintzu, she didn't with him. And the moment he noticed that he was shunned, he jumped to his feet from his chair as if he'd been burned, and I don't know what he would have said—he would have made a fool of himself insulting her, or he would have let himself be humiliated by her—if there hadn't entered on him ("entered" is the right word here) the weeping of Pecker's son-in-law, at the same time as the son-in-law himself.

"Did something get under your skin, a nail or something?" Longbarrel attacked him first.

"Tsk."

"Did you swallow a tack?"

"Tsk."

"Then why the Goddamn hell are you howling like someone bitten by a snake?"

"Died."

"Who, the bride?"

"Him."

"Who's him, Pecker?"

"Him. He jumped into the well to drink water and . . ."

"Wasn't he tied up?"

"He broke his ties and ran toward the well shouting: Water! Water! And then he plunged into it head first."

"Did you pull him out?"

"No, we can't: He won't take hold of the ropes nor of the pole we hold out for him to grab onto, and nobody has the nerve to go in after him—don't want to get bitten."

"Let's go see," said Danila.

"No use: by now he's drowned to death," said Moses.

"From Pecker's to here is about two kilometers. By the time the son-in-law got here, he was dead."

"He didn't die," said the son-in-law to Moses.

"Didn't you say that he was dead?"

"He didn't die during the time I came here, because I wouldn't have left him there alive to come after the doctor; he died when I was there, he came up to the surface, belly up."

"So what do you need a doctor for now? Go get the priest," Longbarrel threw out at him.

"My mother-in-law has gone for the priest."

"Come on, let's go," proposed Horia Dunarintzu.

"Come on, I'm going too," put in Cowskinner, who had appeared immediately after the son-in-law, attracted by the weeping.

"Come along, who's stopping you?"

"Longbarrel, don't talk to me like that. I want to show you something . . . Come see, only I beg Miss Firulescu not to come . . . Let me show you my horse."

"To hell with the horse," said the son-in-law.

"You've never seen anything like this before . . . Doctor, he's had his rod burning for two days," he whispered to Danila.

And when Florentine went into the clinic, Cowskinner gave them all a push from behind toward the stable, and no one protested too strongly—when you came down to it, they didn't have any reason to hurry, Pecker was gone.

He said: "His funnel stays up and he stomps on his hooves, he's tied up, and neighs hoarsely, and beats himself on the belly with it."

He was walking with a lantern in front of him. The horse was tied up under the shed next to the stable, and Cowskinner shined the light on the part he wanted to show them, and I don't know who laughed, maybe even Cowskinner. "It stays as stiff as wood," he laughed.

And I, having come closer to them next to the eaves of the house, saw his face lighted up by the lantern, looking proud that he had such an animal. And it seems to me that it was Horia Dunarintzu who said:

"Incredible!"

"It's incredible, yes," agreed Cowskinner. "They've never seen anything like this in Paris."

"No, something else is incredible!"

"What?"

But Horia Dunarintzu, or whoever it was who had spoken (there was a lot of racket and it was pretty far away from me, and night had fallen and it was hard for me to tell who it was) never answered what was incredible, and they all thought it was the horse's vigor. But I was convinced, and still am, that he wanted to say that it was incredible how the death of a person wasn't an event anymore, even if he died rabid and drowned, and that instead, what was interesting was Cowskinner's steed's pizzle which everybody was staring at.

I got to Pecker before them, and Big Prince told me to go in after the dead man; to go into the well on my stilts and let myself go sliding down them, after untying them from my feet, with the lantern in hand, and put two pieces of rope under the drowned man, and then in between put a meter-long board (that he had there in his hands) as a kind of bed so they would be able to pull him up to the surface without breaking, God forbid, an arm or a leg, and when they pulled him up to the ground from underground where he was soaking in the water, I was to slip under the dead man and watch from underneath so that he wouldn't get scratched on the face or hands from the cement casing of the well. And so I went in exactly as he said, and only after the dead man started to be pulled up, with me under him and the water running down from his clothes onto me, and the lantern I had went out on me, only after that was I overcome with terror. My legs shook and felt as if they might give way, and I wasn't firm on my stilts anymore, and the yells of the people at the mouth of the well, and their faces bent toward the dead man and toward me and illuminated slantwise by the lantern, and the wetness of the cement behind me, and the horror that the dead man might slip between the ropes and fall back on me and take me with him to the bottom of the well—all that, and other things too, made me yell. And my yelling sounded so horrifying in the well that it horrified me even more; but those who were pulling up the ropes were even more confused, and maybe they thought it was the resurrected dead man yelling, and let the ropes go loose some, and Pecker got through a wide part and fell head first into the water next to me, as if he wanted to drown himself a second time, and he took me along with him too, and I swallowed water, and surfaced yelling, and grabbed my stilts, and looked up and saw Pecker's feet hanging in the ropes for a moment, then I didn't see them anymore, and didn't see anyone anymore at the mouth of the well: they had all fled at the sound of my voice, which maybe up there sounded thick and hoarse like Pecker's when he was alive and rabid. And left alone there, I got back my courage all at once and told myself: what can you do, there's nothing to be scared of, those bastards let go. And I didn't yell anymore, I started calling out their names: "Prince! Milksop! Booodea! Zapirtzaaan! Ostrogoooooth!" But they didn't answer me and ran away from the backyard thinking that death was calling to them. Lereu told me that he met them running; they thought I had croaked too, and that the water was out for their heads next.

8

Tanned my hide—that's what Danila did to me with
the belt he was wearing around his waist; he whacked me
on my bare bottom and my back and my legs, and I saw
how my skin got wavy with black and blue welts, and
how blood was about to come out, but didn't flow because
it seemed scared of the other whacks that would come
down on it in torrents, one on top of the other, and if it
came out it would have had to drain out of me from all
the blows I took. And what really got me was that Lereu
didn't jump up to protect me, which showed that half of
the thrashing I got really came from him too. Everybody
was minding his own business, and my shrieks, swallowed inside of me, groaned and not shrieked, made only
Florentine take my side. And the result was that she too
got a smack on the hands when she came up to take me
away from Danila, but all she said was:
   "Are you rabid?"
   "Go take care of your hairdo, keep out of this."
   But she didn't go home with Longbarrel after that, she
went back with us to the clinic. Me they put in Moses'
buggy, half dead as I was, and at the clinic Danila gave me
several blows once again, terrible, so that I felt how my
flesh was freezing, as if it wasn't mine anymore but someone else's put on top of me, burning hot, like a blanket.
But the whole time I was having my hide tanned with the
belt, I didn't feel any fear at all; I didn't feel the terror that
had darkened the inside of me like death, and had dried up
my throat so that I felt the air passing through my gullet,
harsh, like sandpaper on sandpaper, scraping, weak, almost all gone so that I was screaming to get it inside of
me. I wasn't afraid, and I could even say that the whacks

produced a kind of tickling in me that made me laugh—
and this made Danila even angrier. He was making
mincemeat out of me, and I was happy that he was beating me, and that silly happiness and my laughter couldn't
have expressed anything except those horrible moments I
spent in the well with Pecker next to me, and with his
eyes popping out at me. They pulled him out too, I don't
know how, after they pulled me out, shoving in a ladder
that had been lengthened, and Lereu coming down on it
to me. Once out, I didn't have time to say boo before
Danila got at me, first taking the snot out of me with his
hands before pulling the belt off his waist. He made my
bottom so raw that when my folks arrived, snarling and
snapping their teeth and ready to knock out mine for
having gone into the well, at the sight of me they started
weeping with pity, then shouted that Danila should go to
hell, and shouted him out of there.

"And you, Lereu, what do you have to say about him
killing my child? Why did you let him, Lereu!"

"Huh?"

"Why did you, you . . . ?"

"He's one hell of a guy, that doctor!" said Lereu with
admiration.

But my folks didn't understand why Danila was one
hell of a guy: because he was beating me, or becuase he
couldn't be beaten by Lereu? And much later Lereu told
me why he had said: "He's one hell of a guy, that doctor"—because only someone who was one hell of a smart
guy could do what he did: make me burn from being
beaten so that I sent him to hell, and then feel sorry for
me afterwards and treat my wounds, which is what happened; and I wouldn't think anymore about anything except his belt, and not dream about anything except it,
which is what happened. I dreamed about him bending
over me with the belt raised up in the air, hissing toward
me . . . yes, that's what he wanted: for me not to think
about the cold darkness in the well and the dead man who
was dripping wet, and not to dream about Pecker falling

on me every night, wet, with his head hanging down and his eyes popping out. That's why the doctor was one hell of a guy. And not only for that: by him beating me out of my senses one time, I not only got out of the beating my folks would have given me the next day anyhow when they had found out, (and it would have been a senseless beating because that very night I would have started to dream about Pecker), but I also got out of the other beatings my folks would have given me so that I wouldn't go into a well ever again (although for sure I'd never have gone into a well ever again, even under torture), so it saved me from those pointless smacks and whacks and strappings. Because, according to Lereu, how could they ever beat a child they had to pity, especially when they had someone else, the doctor, to vent their anger on? As for me, I became pure and innocent, maybe just because I had been so dumb as to go in after Pecker. And the whole time I was taking the strapping from Danila, Longbarrel was sobbing.

"You crying because you're sorry for him?" Moses asked him, curious.

"Nope."

"Because you're sorry Pecker died?"

"Nope," said Longbarrel.

"Why would he cry about Pecker's dying?" put in Miss Florentine Firulescu. "He didn't drown, he was drowned!"

"What do you mean?" Moses gave a start.

"He was tied up and had no way of escaping, even if he had been a bull. Then too, no matter how often they'd hold out the water jug to him, he'd never go near it, and I'd say that in those moments he groaned even more fiercely and his hands trembled with fury and his pulse quickened (I took his pulse, I wasn't afraid of getting rabies) and he gnashed his teeth that he kept clamped together all the time so that no liquid could be somehow forced down his throat, and his fixed look had a gleam of madness about it (he was syphilitic, I told you), and in him you could clearly see what terror is. It gave you the goose bumps to look at him and see that if a cup of water can cause such terror in a person then the tortures I've heard about that other people have been subjected to must have driven not only them out of their minds, but also those who watched them, their torturers."

"Oh Lord above!" Longbarrel bowed down, and then got up on a chair to reach the cardboard icon tacked up next to the window, and he kissed it several times in a row. Then he took the lantern from the porch and ran to Cowskinner's stable.

"He got drunk on the *tzuica* that was left on the table," said Danila, wrapping me in a wet sheet (my folks hadn't come yet).

"Miss, don't get sidetracked," said Moses, "how come you say Pecker was drowned?"

"Okay: there was somebody who couldn't stand to have rabies in the house and have the family be made a laughing stock—because now even the disease, if real, is considered by some to be an out and out disgrace. And since there was no hope for his recovery, that person loosened his ties, and when the others went to bed, took him lightly by the scruff of the neck and pulled him out—and Pecker let him, thinking that he was escaping from the coop, seeing himself free—and then caught him by surprise and threw him head first into the well."

"That's what you think?"

"Yes, doctor. He was killed; people have managed to get so thoroughly scared of rabies that they even believe in it and kill innocent people in order to escape from it."

"That's your view?"

"Yes, doctor. Because this much you know too, that if Pecker really did have rabies, he would never under any circumstances have dared to go near a well, even if he was free."

"He was tortured by thirst," said Moses.

"He was tortured by thirst, but whenever he saw water, which could have relieved the burning inside of him, he didn't dare touch it, and what's more, the closer the water jug got to him, the more it terrified him."

"You're right," said Danila.

"Are you joking?"

"No, you're right: Pecker had rabies!"

"I didn't say that!"

"Then what did you say, Miss?"

"That he was so horrified by water that he couldn't have gone to the well to fling himself in it."

"Exactly, rabies!"

"No, doctor. I'm saying that he didn't throw himself into the water, it terrified him and, although he wanted to quench his thirst, he would never have dared even to dream of drinking water."

"Right, he never would have dared, but don't foregt that he was in a state where you really can't talk about daring anymore; he was no longer conscious. There's no question of a crime, the man died purely and simply by flinging himself into a well in a moment of unconsciousness."

"You'd pay any price to be right, wouldn't you?"

"Miss, I personally don't care one way or the other if he was killed or if he killed himself, that's somebody else's problem, and not even yours. For us, for me and for you, the only problem is: was it the rabies virus or not? And although you fly off the handle at me when you're playing detective, what you're saying comes to exactly what I myself maintain."

"I don't think so."

"Exactly the same; except that you maintain it couldn't be suicide—you also exclude the possibility of an accident, since you want absolutely for him to have been killed!—because he was horrified, terrorized by water, you said, but I say that that horror is a specific symptom . . ."

"Doctor!" called Cowskinner in a whisper, "come and see how Longbarrel is looking at himself with the lantern and at the horse."

But the doctor didn't have to go—the discussion with Miss Firulescu was broken off—because Longbarrel came right up to us, bowing down: "Oh Lord, Oh my God, Oh Lord above, save me! Doctor, doctor . . . Miss, for pity's sake . . . only us . . ."

And she understood and left to go see Cowskinner's wife.

"What is it, you?" Cowskinner was curious, "What's got into you?"

"Doctor, I . . . like . . . the horse . . ."

"What?" asked Danila.

"That."

"You go to hell, you're just the way you've always been since you were born," laughed Cowskinner. "You keep acting like a fool."

"No, no, it's stayed like this for two days."

"And before?"

"From time to time, maybe half a day, but now it's been two full days, and I wouldn't have known what it was if I hadn't seen the horse."

"Come on, let's see," laughed Cowskinner.

"You've got the devil in you and I . . ."

"Go to Margherita," laughed Cowskinner.

"I was there all morning. No good."

"Go again."

"Come on, let's go see," said Danila, but he didn't leave, he couldn't; my folks came and right away all hell broke loose.

The priest from Patirlagele didn't come to the funeral; he was called to Bucharest about some icons, or he left so as not to be home for Pecker's burial—there was still talk about him having thrown himself into the well, and if that was the case, the priest didn't want to chant for his last journey or let him be put into the cemetery ground. Those who take their own life, which is given to them by God, by their own free will, don't deserve the service of the church (they belong to Satan). In any case, whether he was called to Bucharest or not, it was better for the priest

to be absent; that way he was not obliged even to accept
having Pecker carried through the cemetery gates, nor to
have to refuse him the services of the church, or maybe
this way he gave the dead man the opportunity to have an
eternal place on the hillside next to his relatives, and to
be chanted to by a priest from farther away, if they could
find one. However, the son-in-law didn't even try to find
one; Bitza was there in the village, and she knew the
whole service of the dead ever since the war when she
chanted it in the houses of those who had fallen far away.
And now she chanted for Pecker, and even if she didn't
have a censer, the smell of incense filled the rooms, burning in old teacups filled with corncob embers; and the
smell was the important thing, not the censer. Bitza
prayed nasally—so as to sound like the voice of a priest—
that Pecker be accepted into heaven, and prayed that all
the edges of the earth sigh for the miserable Pecker to
whom a cruel judgment from up in heaven had come: to
have his hands and feet tied, and to be cast out of life and
out of the world. And because Bitza hadn't acted as a
priest since the war, since when there was no priest anywhere in the area, everybody remembered those who had
fallen, or who had died without leaving a trace, in foreign
lands, and the grief was so great that the whole village
wept all the way to Pecker's grave, everyone weeping in
fact for his own dead, who weren't there, and whom they
didn't even hope, really, to see ever again. Only Miss Florentine Firulescu didn't shed a tear, and I realized afterwards that she not only hated useless tears, but especially
hated suffering in the face of someone who had been defeated by death, and couldn't bear, except with a faint
sarcastic smile at the corners of her lips, the whole dead
man's journey from the house he was leaving to the house
of earth he was moving to, since she detested death and
was somehow proud that other people's useless grief
couldn't touch her. And she was right to be like that,
since for her, not being from the village or related to anyone, death couldn't take on the appearance of someone

close to her and be seen in him, since death usually takes on the image of the dead person. For her, death was anonymous, and from that came her almost inhuman indifference; and you couldn't condemn her for it, and I couldn't blame her either, since even at the time when Bitza performed the service of the dead to the clothes placed on a bed of someone who had died at the front, and I couldn't see that person's face and didn't even know him except by name (having been too little when he left), the whole thing back then seemed ridiculous to me. But now it was all different: death was called Pecker and he had his eyes closed, eyes that once looked at me alive and merry, and alive and clouded in the well. But not only for me was Bitza's chanting more filled with chills this time: he who had gained the light of the world, as she said, and who was to dwell in the grave, there where emperors together with rich men may be seen, was Pecker, dressed in the bridegroom's black suit and with the bridegroom's tie and hat on. He never thought he would be leaving, carried out on other people's shoulders so soon, and he hadn't had a suit made for himself, but he was lucky that his son-in-law's clothes fit him. So, he lay in the coffin, all stiff, with his hands folded on his chest, like a bridegroom, and Bitza:

"Him whom You moved from the face of the earth, You whose lordly power we praise, take him to You, make him a son of light and wash away his veil of sins."

And already I saw Pecker shining in paradise, which was the place where you went from the grave they'd dug, out to another world, into another village, shining from head to toe and alive once again and cleaned of rabies. Pecker was moving from Braniste to another Braniste, that was it, and there wasn't any way you could keep yourself from weeping over a man who would never return, despite the fact that here, as Bitza chanted, he had gained the world of light and satisfied all his desires.

And said Bitza: "When we gain the world of light, then dwell we in the grave."

If Pecker had known that, he never would have married

off his daughter; it was better not to gain anything and not to have to move. They wept over him much more than over their own dead, and his death was more horrifying than the whole war that had ended and that didn't have a face—it was made only out of Bitza's services and memorials. It would have been even better if the war hadn't ended, at least for those of my age; memorials were held one after the other, and we got out of school to go to them. You'd eat and drink, and only those from the household would cry at the beginning until the bottles would pile up, and then everybody would forget why they were gathered together, or they didn't forget and got drunk out of anger, and once they were drunk they started not believing in death. That's how it was. They didn't believe in it and started singing the departed one's songs, and cursing. Now nobody was cursing, and things looked more serious than before; anyone could die, not only men who were away from home, there wasn't even a front anymore as the only place where a person could die suddenly; now everybody was weeping for Pecker, as if each of them was weeping for himself.

Only Miss Firulescu walked along, indifferent, and not even at the cemetery did she stop telling Danila her opinion in a loud voice, paying no attention to anybody around her, and not even to the dead man who went in front of her, carried on other people's shoulders, and not even to the fact that she was passing over dead people and was walking among them or even on top of them. She was saying with a loud mouth what she had said earlier at the clinic, and the doctor was listening to her with one ear, or he wasn't listening at all, and she didn't even give a damn if he was listening to her or not, since she wasn't talking only for him; she had gotten hoarse; it had to be known that it wasn't rabies, and that the dead man had been murdered. She stumbled against a clump of grass and the heel of her shoe fell off and she threw the shoe down on the ground in a fury and then picked it up and just walked on with one shoe off, right after Pecker, supporting herself on Danila's arm, running off at the mouth above those who were lamenting wordlessly, and above those of us who were down below. And Danila was in seventh heaven because, although she was contradicting him (without his even answering, since she was continuing the discussion begun at the clinic), she was leaning against him, she needed him, at least up to the grave, or until they went out of the cemetery, or until they got to her house, and that discovery excited him and made his cheeks flush. And later when I remembered their walking together and was sure that it was a recognition of love, at least for him at that time, that he couldn't live without her nor her without him, I was filled with bitterness, because that discovery of his, that she was indispensable to him, was made in Pecker's funeral procession, among the evergreen trees beside the crosses on the graves. I think I was convinced all along, and still am today, that this moment was the beginning of the end for Danila. He took Florentine to her room at Ostrogoth's, and since she had scraped the sole of her foot on the edge of a tile, he washed her feet, kneeling in front of her like an idiot who has lost his mind or who doesn't know what it means to wash someone's feet. I watched them through the window from our house; he wanted to get the sand out of the scrape but couldn't, and she was looking straight at the top of his head and didn't seem surprised that he didn't succeed in cleaning the wound, and it seemed that he didn't even want to finish washing her feet ever; and both were stupefied and kept telling each other what should be done so that she wouldn't get tetanus, and it was clear, at least to me, that they couldn't live without each other anymore. Nevertheless, I repeat, I will always see how Danila didn't have a fir tree beside his cross, and didn't even have a cross, because he discovered, there among the trees, how loneliness had died in him and how he couldn't live without her anymore, although he could die without her. When I saw him with his hands in the basin of water, washing every toe on her foot, I went to pieces laughing that he could be so dumb in front of a girl or a woman, and I had to laugh, and kept on laughing, because when I was leaving the cemetery on stilts, passing over crosses and flowers and coming to the bushes next to the cemetery, I saw Longbarrel there in the underbrush, grinding down on Margherita until, after a while, she started struggling and hitting him wildly all over, and then she pushed him aside by kneeing him in the belly and ran off through the young willows toward the village, gathering her hair up into her kerchief as she went. But Longbarrel, unsatisfied and crying, went out of the bushes onto the road, and since people were going home from the dead, he winked at Bitza, who then tore herself away from the women and went into the underbrush by a different path than the one where Longbarrel was half hidden, and they met up not long after in the tall bushes near the ravine where people sometimes went to get sand for the foundations of houses, and she sat down and I couldn't see her anymore, and he was covered with bushes that shaded her, and for a while I didn't hear anything except the wind blowing through the thick leaves of the young willows, and after that I heard Bitza chanting as if to the dead in a priestly way, nasally, performing:

"With His feathers you will shade yourself, and you will have no fear of ghosts in the night or of flying arrows in the day. And on His hands will you be raised, so that no stone will your foot strike against . . ."

"Amen," said Longbarrel.

And Bitza: "Now to my mind has been recalled the prophet who cried out: Earth and ashes am I; and again and again have I looked into graves and seen bare bones and said: verily, who here is the emperor, who the soldier, who the rich man, who the poor man?" And since Longbarrel remained silent, Bitza said to him: "Say Amen, you creep!"

"Amen."

And Bitza went on chanting everything she had chanted beside Pecker.

9

Still, I think I did know Kalagherovich; by sight; in any case I did see him. If by some chance he was that man who came looking for Dunarintzu during the time of the rains in July. There was an autumn cold snap and the sky was dark and the birds didn't even sing anymore except in the intervals between the rains. Rain after rain fell day and night, enough to rot even the roses that were blooming. One afternoon a person appeared riding a bicycle, dripping wet, and after he had gone up and down the streets looking for Dunarintzu, he stopped at the clinic, where he found him taking shelter from the rain with Moses. That day Miss Florentine hadn't served them anything. All three were watching the rain and waiting for it to clear so that the two men could leave for Patirlagele and she for the hairdresser in Cimpuletz. It was Thursday. I had come to have Danila dress my wounds where he had beaten me, and since he wasn't there I didn't let Miss Firulescu touch me and said I would wait for him, and I waited more to be with them than to have the doctor put ointment on me. And I came to him only so he could see that I wasn't angry at him for beating me. The linden trees were in full bloom, and for something to do, I tore off a branch from Cowskinner's linden, broken by the wind, and started to gather the flowers and spread them out on a table to dry. When it wasn't raining, I was in the habit of picking flowers from the lindens from up on my stilts wherever I happened to find them, and would stuff them in my shirt and go around the village with them, fragrant at my breast. Especially in the morning, and especially when the sun was shining limpid and white and not hot or torpid. All the lindens seemed to be illuminated by a light that came from within them, from their glowing flowers. When it rained, their fragrance was insipid and also damp and faint, and I didn't like it. Kalagherovich, or the man who could have been Kalagherovich, the one who came on the bicycle, after shaking hands with the poeple next to me, shook hands with me too, and that astounded me because I never would have thought that a full-grown man would ever shake hands with a kid. It It was hardly usual; no, it wasn't usual at all.

Dunarintzu said to him: "Good cheer." And: "What's happened?"

"Nothing. I came to see you."

If for sure he was Kalagherovich, they would have had to be surprised that he was there, free, with his bicycle in Braniste. Or maybe they knew that he wasn't where he had been anymore, or maybe they had already met. They talked about the Danube, that it had rained a lot up there—in other countries, up there—and that the water had carried off beehives and the trunks of trees, chairs, and hope chests; it had taken everything. Then along came Longbarrel, holding his jaws, rocking his head in pain; Sevastitza had also cut him under the tongue, to kill the worms hidden there in the strings of the under tongue, and he couldn't talk from the pain, but murmured through his nose. He was nevertheless happy that Sevastitza had, by cutting, saved him from the disease you got from worms or from the "little dogs" that grew rabid under the tongue; the bad blood had flowed away, he had seen it go with his own eyes, and in fact, he had come to Cowskinner's now to cut the stallion in the stable under the tongue with a razor to see if afterwards he would still have such a furious limb. He had also brought a demijohn of *tzuica* to get the horse dead drunk so he wouldn't somehow bite him. And since Cowskinner was in Turnuvechi and Longbarrel couldn't talk, we realized what he wanted to do only after seeing the horse turned over in the dirt, motionless; Longbarrel had tied his legs with rope and was almost choking him with a noose around his neck, and was pouring *tzuica* from the demijohn between his jaws which he had tied together, but with a piece of wood wedged in between. The stallion wasn't struggling. The *tzuica* had been mixed with pure alcohol and had a very quick effect; or maybe not; in any case, he was so strangled by the tether that Longbarrel didn't even need to waste the drink on him to make him stay still. I think he was already dead—choked—when Longbarrel was pouring *tzuica* down his throat and cutting him under the tongue with the razor. Still, some blood flowed, but the stallion never got up off the ground again. He died, however, with his pizzle in full power.

The rain stopped and Florentine asked Kalagherovich— if that was Kalagherovich—for his bicycle so that she could go around the village, and didn't wait for him to say yes or no but went off on it and was gone. (After a few hours she came back from Cimpuletz, not Braniste; she had gotten her hair done.) I'll never know for sure if that man was Kalagherovich or not, since, I forgot to tell you, Sevastitza changed everybody's name to protect them from the rabies demon, as she put it, and so that the evil spirit wouldn't be able to find them and stick to them. I know that she christened me Balta and everybody knew my new name before I did, and I found it out only after; Longbarrel was called Bargain, Lereu—George, Margherita—Sweetie, Ostrogoth—Sofronie, Milksop—Zabic, Little Prince—Hitler, Bitza—Evangeline, Danila— Acatrinei, Florentine—Mia, Moses—Cazan, and so on; everybody had a different name so that neither dogs nor disease would recognize them. When the person with the bicycle came, everybody had changed names and people didn't call each other by their real names anymore, and even those who didn't believe in giving nicknames still didn't call people they met by their true name so as not to make them angry; maybe those people they met were believers, and to say their name would mean revealing their identity to the mysterious and terrifying disease.

Not even in fun did they ever call each other by their old names, even if some of them used the new names only jokingly. Rabies had no beginning and no end and could have an ear anywhere, said Sevastitza, and once it got into a person it twisted about in him, unaffected by any sort of doctor's doctoring and came to rule over the blood and the breath of that person until it snuffed them out and went to rule over another person. And if it heard, let's say Longbarrel's new name—Bargain, it wouldn't touch Longbarrel but someone somewhere who happened to have the name of Bargain. So that if someone, I don't know who, called the man with the bicycle Kalagherovich, it's not certain that it was Kalagherovich; he could have changed his name and gotten christened with that one so as to ward off the disease and drive it to the person with the other name.

"Here comes Acatrinei," said Moses (Cazan), pointing to Danila. (I forgot to tell you: Horia Dunarintzu was given the name of Lawrence by the old woman).

"Where's Miss . . . ?" was Acatrinei's first question.

"She went out riding on this man's bicycle. Let me introduce you. Our doctor from Braniste, Kalagherovich."

Acatrinei (I'll have to talk about them with their new names, just as it was then, so you'll understand how it really was, if anybody can understand anything here) bristled, and you could see that it didn't give him any pleasure to be introduced to the owner of the bicycle, who said:

"I just happened by here, I have to be going, I don't want to bother you."

"But you're not disturbing me in the least."

"Thanks anyway, but still I have to leave. I wouldn't want to cause you any inconvenience in the future."

"I don't understand," Acatrinei almost blew up at him.

"I don't know if you've heard of me."

"Sir, please have a seat and don't put me in a difficult position, first of all in my own eyes. Whoever you may be, you are here at the clinic, in other words in my house, and

I'm not throwing you out; I'm not afraid either of you or of others."

"Why should you be afraid?" the man with the bicycle didn't understand and smiled.

"Let's just skip it," Cazan intervened. "See doctor, that child came to have his wounds treated."

"He can wait," he scowled at me.

But I didn't get mad; I knew he was thinking about Miss Mia and was scowling for that reason. Nevertheles, he put something on my bruises—it was pure water, I think, so that I wouldn't say he didn't put anything—and he gave me a smack on the bottom and told me:

"Get lost!"

I went out onto the road and went into Kitchea's (Bodea's) garden, and then went from the roof of Jeremy's (Cowskinner's) stable to the roof of the storehouse (nobody was home) and from there, through a hole in the roof, I could see and hear them on the porch of the clinic. Bargain, who was drunk from all he had swilled from the demijohn, was sleeping on his back, snoring, on duty next to the stallion, whom the flies were swarming on.

"I'm glad that you're friends," Cazan told the man with the bicycle, "and that you've come to see him (he pointed to Lawrence, that is, to your father). That explains why he cared about you and wouldn't say a word against you."

"That's why I came to see him: to tell him to talk, if it still might be necessary."

"Why?"

"In order to live. What sense is there in stretching out the chain and his coming beside me, and after him to have someone else dragged into this chain of people? The chain must be broken, he must say whatever he's asked to."

"You mean lie?"

"Of course."

"But don't you think somebody will notice that they're lies?"

"Sure. But that's what they want: lies."

"They won't believe him."

"Yes they will, they'll believe him all right, precisely because they don't believe him and they don't believe him because they know the truth, and if they don't actually know it they feel it. However, they don't have time anymore to shed light on the matter, and they don't even need to, what they need is people who will pay for their stupidities—which is the case of your friend, Galatioan."

"He's not my friend."

"Oh, you'd better not say that again. He might hear you."

"Why are you arguing with me?"

"I'm not arguing. I'm telling you what I think—since I'm sure that you'll tell him."

"Then that means that you came to see me and not him (and he pointed to your father) doesn't it?"

"Both of you. I want to tell you that you can tell Galatioan that I know why he set me free: so he could see where I would go and who I would meet with, what I would talk about, what I would plot, what connections I have, what people I know; and this isn't just for me, they know all they need to know about me; they want to see who they can get into trouble so as to get at me better by getting at them. I know; and it's precisely because I know that now I should stay shut up in my house and not see anybody and not endanger anybody, that I'm not staying shut up in my house, thinking that it's worth it, because for me there's no place left on earth, none—I keep moving; and I came to see you two because you're exactly what I'm looking for."

"But don't put us two in the same boat."

"But it's perfectly natural, my friend."

(I've thought many times about whether that man was Kalagherovich; the story was very much like his, but that's exactly why he could have been someone else.)

"Doctor, since you were so kind as to offer me a chair, wouldn't you like to be even kinder and leave us alone for a while? There's no reason for you to be involved in such a dirty business."

"What are you talking about?"

"Precisely because you don't know, it would be better for you not to find out."

"But hearing something doesn't seem to me to be a crime."

"On the contrary, it is a crime. I mean, you yourself could be one of the victims."

"You've got only dumb things in your head, Kalagherovich," said Cazan, not losing the smile that he was never without.

"No sir, I'm not afraid, but I'm leaving because you've asked me to and I don't want to be a boor."

Danila left, and I believed him that he didn't take off out of fear, but I was also sure that he went off so readily so as to see where Miss Mia was riding on the bicycle.

"You said that I had only dumb things in my head. If that were so, then it would be bad only for me. But you're scared of talking to me too, although you don't have any reason to be; or maybe you ought to have a reason to be happy, because from me you've got some evidence that you can transmit to your friend. But, you're afraid even of this evidence, which is in your favor, since you're not sure that tomorrow he won't get angry with you and blame you for talking to a person as rotten and dangerous as a disease, who might have infected you too, and made you become dangerous."

"You're exaggerating, as always."

"Really?"

"The fact that you're here means that there is a principle of justice, which is not influenced by your words and which is above your person; I mean, it isn't frightened by you or by what you say. The world is changed, it is steadier on its feet and can't be knocked over by a person of whom it is said, and rightly so, that he's only interested in his own career, and that he considers anyone else's position to be a slap against his career."

"I see that you're up to date: I'm a careerist. I've admitted that, whenever I was asked to."

"You see, anything that doesn't suit you, you sneer at."

"No, dear friend. The facts speak for themselves. I've always said that I wanted to be boss of everything in the Turnuvechi area, which includes both Cimpuletz and Braniste, where we are now. On my word of honor, even now I want to be boss, I say it with all my heart. And I think I'll make it. When, however, I don't know exactly."

"You said you came to see him but you've been talking only to me. Am I so dear to you?"

"Very dear, because I don't understand you. What made you side with Galatioan? Why did you sign a blank check to what he thinks? For seven minutes of sweet sleep? Why are you taking the cheapest path, the restful path, the way filled with sleep? Out of laziness or from a kind of viciousness that I never suspected was in you?"

"I am vicious, Kalagherovich," he smiled. "But you, why are you playing the great apostle when you curse everything around you, how can you play the communist?"

"Because I am one."

"You think so?"

"I do, yes."

"Then what are you crying about, why are you playing the victim?"

"My dear friend, I'm not playing the victim, I am a victim."

"Ho, ho!" Cazan laughed heartily. "You see, I don't understand you either, so we're even."

"It's normal for you not to understand me; after all, we think differently."

"You're a braggart and, by God, I believe you when you say that you're a careerist. You want to make a sensation, gain fame among the people as a man who says 'no' and who, like a saint, wants only good. It's very easy, by God, Kalagherovich!"

"Then why don't you try to do like me? Find out how pleasant it is inside when the door slams and it's slamming on you; it's delightful, why don't you try it?"

"Poor you, how you've suffered! You don't want to make me cry, do you?"

"No, God forbid! It would be so very hard for me to make you cry, and it would be ridiculous too for you to cry, a strong man like you! You don't even have a reason to cry; I could be ridiculous if I cried, but you couldn't even be that."

"Why would you cry, Kalagherovich; because you missed something?"

"What did I miss?"

"The train."

"It's not a question of trains with me. Trains come and go, and if you miss one, you've missed the business or the pleasure at the place where it would have taken you, but you can wait for another train to take you, a little late, to the same business or to another. I haven't missed any train, because I wasn't waiting for any train."

"What did you sign up for, long ago?"

"Not for trains."

"Maybe you believe that now it's different from the way you imagined it when you joined in the game?"

"For me it's the same."

"Even though you're out now?"

"I didn't take myself out, they threw me out."

"To hell with all this, why don't you admit that if you didn't miss the train, you lost the game."

"I didn't lose anything."

"Maybe you're ashamed of breaking with what you've done and saying that you're wrong and that you should start your life over from the beginning."

"That's what you'd like: for me to confess that I'm not what I am. No, under no circumstances. Look, here's the nurse."

She was coming on the bicycle with her hair done, and in front of her, where children sit, was the doctor, between her hands that were holding tight to the handlebars. They went whizzing by the gate without stopping, waving.

"How about admitting that you were in contact with Policarp Ionascu?"

"I've admitted everything that was asked of me."

"And it wasn't true?"

"I don't like to remember pain from the past everyday; it would mean becoming an accomplice to the people who made me feel the pain. I didn't want to act when I could have, and not even when I had the right to, and make that sergeant—the one who pulled out my nails—answer for what he did, and pay him back what he deserved, and pay myself, and in that way be paid, at a fair price, what was my due; but there's no price for something like that and I didn't lift a finger to get acquitted; that would have meant that everything I thought before had, as its purpose, a price and not a reason for being; no, I wasn't waiting for any train, and afterwards, I didn't take the smallest step against that sergeant who, by a strange coincidence, lives right on my street, because I have a horror of the notion of victim, and would never have wanted to avenge myself using the same coin as he, and in so doing to become his equal, and implicitly their equal; because it wasn't out of his head that came the idea of doing to me what you can still see today. I even requested to move from Bolintineanu Street so as not to make him move, and so that I wouldn't have to see him anymore and be reminded every day that he exists and that he was able to do what he was told to do and therefore that man is sometimes so base that he can do anything he is asked to do. I heard that, by a quirk of fate, or because of negligence on his part, or maybe it was his destiny always and forever to be a prison guard, he's still working in prison today, and my horror of being imprisoned is so great because I'll meet up with him again and he'll smile at me again in a superior way, and with justice on his side, being on the outside of the prison cells, and I won't be able to fulfill my obligation anymore, not having a single healthy toenail."

"You're almost a saint."

"That's just what he said to me long ago, when he bandaged my feet. Don't make me remember it all, it's very easy for me to do, and for that reason very difficult. You mentioned Policarp. Yes, I was in contact with Policarp Ionascu. My wife had to hear and learn that I was Policarp's man and, faced with my own confession, which they demanded so as to inform her of this, she had to believe I was guilty; this small point was my hope; that she would believe I was Policarp's man, in other words that I was on the side of the man who, above all others, was also the initiator of, if not exactly the responsible one for, my nails—I'll only mention them, they can't be seen. If I hadn't admitted what they demanded, they still would have found evidence to prove that I was one with Policarp, and the first proof, they told me themselves, would have been gotten from my wife; how, I could imagine very clearly! And rather than bringing her where I myself was, and leaving the children with nobody, I preferred to resolve everything more quickly with one humiliation and a blow only to myself."

"They beat you again, poor man, and so as not to have to endure the whip—the whip, right?—you told them what they demanded."

"No, it wasn't that simple. Not right after being beaten; a beating can be borne, it makes you fight back, it makes you rebel—one can see that you lack experience, you've never suffered—and you don't give in. I started to waiver when the hissing got to be too much for me. Then I told myself: if my family escapes, everything is okay. He understands me better than you do, he has children," he pointed to your father.

"And your wife never believed it."

"No, but it wasn't so very necessary anymore either: I had confessed; they were, I hoped, out of all danger."

"And look how now, with all those confessions, you're free anyway. What you're doing, doesn't it seem awful to you?"

"Sure, talking with you; that's why I tried to find you,

so as to live this painful moment when I would be ridiculous with my story, telling it in front of one of the people who put me there."

"Me?"

"You. Of course you won't admit it, I didn't even expect you to. What I was looking for, I found: for you to smile when I told you where they stuck me and with you-know-who, and for me to feel humiliated again and somehow break myself of the habit of forgiving anymore; that's what I want, to break myself of the habit of thinking that so and so is a good guy!"

"So, you're going to destroy me now."

"I won't be able to, but I can despise you."

"I don't give a damn, Kalagherovich."

"I know, but that's precisely why I want you both here in front of me, so he'll understand what I didn't want to understand: that it's idiotic to believe a man can't be bought, even if he was once your most faithful friend."

"I was bought, huh?"

"Not quite, but you're on your way. And you're doing all you can to be."

"You're such a bore, really. Full of hatred because you didn't reach your goal. Who got money from Policarp, me or you? Who was bought so he would keep machines in his house for clandestine activities?"

"Me."

"Of course you."

"I see you know everything; I give up; they found dollars at my place, and arms and letters, and they discovered the connection I had through Policarp's son with that foreign consul. But enough."

"No, no, Kalagherovich, please continue; weren't you maybe sent here to provoke us? Weren't you maybe even put up to it by Galatioan to see who is on his side and who isn't? Tell everything, so that he can find out too why it's idiotic to believe that man can't be bought. Come on, tell, don't be shy. Maybe even how you never were in prison in the first place (and your nails came off when your feet got frostbitten in the mountain cabin where you got so drunk with Policarp's ex-wife that you couldn't even get out of bed for two days in order to light a fire), and you weren't in prison even now, and the false testimony they demanded of you, you didn't give as dictated by others and only just signed by you, the way you kept saying all over Cimpuletz, but you gave that testimony without going where you said you were so that people would believe you'd suffered and would trust you and tell you what they think, and you'd inform who you're supposed to, and after a time of staying in the shadows, you'd suddenly reappear, bigger than ever, in Turnuvechi, maybe with a higher rank. Do you think I'm so dumb, Kalagherovich, that I swallow all that crap from you? And you don't even allow me to smile, and you want me to believe you when you say that you had some horrible moments in front of me when I laughed at your story and therefore didn't believe you. I wonder why you didn't tell, so he could hear too, everything you told your wife when you got back home— so she wouldn't by some chance think that you weren't in prison; you were instructed to tell that you were imprisoned and beaten and forced to give one piece of information after another—knowing that she has relatives and friends, and that every woman talks about her troubles wherever she finds a listener, and that word about these troubles, real to her but not real in reality, will spread and everybody will find out what a wonderful man you are (a saint! as I've already said); so, I wonder why you didn't tell him too (he has children and would understand you) the lesson you recited to your wife: that after five days and five nights of continuous interrogation and beatings, when you couldn't get back up on your feet unless you got a push, you signed a declaration that was dictated to you, above all to save your wife and children, and the horrible thing was not what you admitted there, but how they, after hammering at you with their fists and questions, always appealed to you as a communist, in other words to your conscience as a Party member, and they told you to help them, for it was precisely your duty to help them crush their enemies. And when you, at the beginning, didn't answer, they assured you that by telling them, you would have the privilege of rehabilitating yourself somehow, that is to say, they would believe first of all that really it was only because of your ill-fated love for Policarp's wife that you got to know him, and they would recognize as honorable that part of your life before Policarp's wife entered the picture, and they would forgive you for everything after you told them frankly what Policarp has been up to for the past several months, and with whom. Come on, Kalagherovich, at least tell him now (because he has children, he understands you) what you told your wife: that you'd be let off from your crimes if you signed. Oh, you really think you're great if you believe you were accused of crimes! Come on, tell him that they told you that you don't love your country and you don't love communism, that's why you're not helping us? Tell how at the end you couldn't hold out anymore, especially when they appealed once again to you as a communist, and you told everything about Policarp Ionascu and your relationship with him. Since you lied to your wife, you can lie to Dunarintzu here too—he's only a friend—and you can assure him that, as a point of fact, you truly never had any relations with Policarp, but you admitted what they asked in order to save your family. And don't let it bother you that there's a discrepancy between the signing of the declaration they asked of you in the name of your being a communist and the fact that such a man would have spoken from the very beginning about having relations with Policarp's wife, and then couldn't have had business relations with him, but if he did have such relations with him (leaving his wife out of it for now), then he wasn't a communist anymore, and they didn't have any reason to appeal to a quality you'd lost long before, if you ever truly had it. The story that you'd be forgiven and that, if you talked, you'd be considered just as pure as before you knew Policarp's wife, isn't true for many reasons, the principal one being that you told your wife that the story about you and Policarp's wife was made up by them and isn't true, but if they knew that the story wasn't true, then they knew that there never existed and never could exist anything before a story that never was; you didn't have a period when you were honest before, since that 'before' is nonexistent; with you everything is uninterrupted, just as Sevastitza says that uninterrupted is rabies once it penetrates into man. But still, it's true about your relationship with Policarp's wife in their winter cabin in Retezat. There you froze, and then you avoided the sergeant from Bolintineanu Street so that they wouldn't find out the truth, that the man you named throughout your autobiography as having pulled out your nails didn't pull them out; you moved to another neighborhood to get a better house, not so as to avoid setting eyes every day on the hangman (!) who reminded you, through his very presence, of the suffering you endured. Why are you so silent, dear friend? You don't use these words, 'dear friend' anymore? Really, is Galatioan so very untruthful when he says that Policarp threw you into prison when he saw that you missed the train, so that you could get out of there as a martyr who could be put in high positions afterwards? And could you possibly consider me such an idiot as to believe that you really came to Braniste to meet him and just to say 'hello' and 'here I am,' and that when you were free you could come on the bicycle (which isn't even yours, because you don't have one) and bump into us, and that you didn't lie to us when you came here out of the blue; you were looking for us! You searched all through Braniste for us or for Kitchea? And you stopped at the clinic to find us or to see Kitchea when he gets home, since he lives almost right next to the clinic? Didn't you really come quickly and sneakily, in a military coat, in this rain that would muffle everything, just to have a word with Kitchea? You were the boss in Cimpuletz before Galatioan, when Kitchea was accidentally caught with some candelabra in his wagon that proved to belong to Policarp's wife (she's divorced from him now). Grilled to find out where he stole them, as was supposed, it was found that he hadn't stolen them, they had been given to him for safe keeping. In them no hidden gold was found, nor any suspicious documents, nothing at all was found; but using them as a point of departure, the man who was being protected was found, for you too know Mrs. Varlaam, as she's now called, by her maiden name. Right Kalagherovich?"

"Right."

"So, don't put on an act for me anymore. You're looking for Kitchea and I can imagine why too. You told your wife a story again, and she, naive that she was, believed you and told both her mother and her Aunt Alexandra, who is a hairdresser in Cimpuletz, and Alexandra told the big mouth nurse who is her friend (and who used to bring her chickens and eggs and tomatoes and wine), and the young woman who is now riding your bicycle knew about you from Alexandra's stories because that miserable Kitchea, with a gun at his head, had testified that you, then the boss in Cimpuletz, were plotting to seize a lot of people in political positions, even Galatioan, your assistant, and throw them into a police van. You wanted, in other words, to pull off a big political coup, through which you could not only get whomever you wanted appointed to key positions, but also you'd be seen in Turnuvechi and higher up as having guts, and would then be given a higher office. You deny all this and say it's trick of Kitchea's to get himself off, and your wife believed you, and I believe you too, however now I wonder: why did you come to talk to Kitchea about a trick? Kalagherovich, your hands aren't clean; either you were put down so that after getting out of where you got out you could then put other people in the jug and climb up on their backs, or actually you planned an even bigger hellish scheme, and in truth you wanted to screw everybody around you and be sent to Turnuvechi, and higher up still. In this whole affair there are a number of points I don't understand, and that's why I believe you're a dangerous man and am discussing this openly with you and even with witnesses. I've said that I'm not a friend of Galatioan's, not because I'm breaking off relations with him in front of you. That would mean I'm coming closer to you and saying that you're in the right. I said I wasn't his friend because I'm not and I don't want to have the word spread that I am, and that I'm using his friendship for I don't know what purpose of my own. Kitchea, however, was a friend of yours, and you even met Mrs. Varlaam several times at night at his house, still coming by bicycle back then although you were a big shot. It was her bicycle. That I found out from Kitchea; when he got out he told me all that, without my asking him, which made me think he was lying. But now I see you with the bicycle. Why did you come? Who are you really? Who you say you are, or who you're telling lies about being, or rather who you are said to be, or are lied about as being?"

10

The bicycle stayed in Braniste, and from morning to night the nurse rode around on it and became so inseparable from it that it was almost impossible to see one of them without the other, and George rightly said that one of them had grown out of the other, the bicycle downwards from her legs and from what the young woman had that pointed to the ground, and the young woman upwards from the bicycle; however the unanswerable question was: which one came first, the woman or the bicycle? The man who had it gave it to Miss Mia as a gift, and she at first had hesitated and had wanted to buy it. But she liked it so much, he observed, that nothing could ever have been enough to pay for it (if, as again George held, the things you buy should be priced, not according to their true value, but according to how much you, the buyer, like them), and so he insisted that she take it as an outright gift, and she thanked him, but not really as much as I would have expected. It even seemed to me that she had expected him to give it to her, since she didn't have a bicycle and deserved to have one. The man who had had it, and who might have been Kalagherovich or might not have been, left here packed into the buggy of Patirlagele's school principal and he was in such a black mood that it seemed to me Miss Mia had done him a favor by taking his bicycle, which otherwise he might have just had to leave in Braniste, sick of riding on it, and in any case, at that time too weak to pedal through the sand over to Cimpuletz. As you can see, I was right when I first told you that I didn't know Kalagherovich; the man I saw back then, coming on the bicycle and leaving without it, I couldn't swear that he was Kalagherovich, but if he was, from the discussions I heard then, I wouldn't be able to say what kind of person he was, and therefore I wouldn't be able to maintain that I knew him. I told the doctor what I had heard ("the whole time I was waiting for you to put salve on me") and he told me he knew all that from his nurse; she had talked to him on the bicycle. Only, Alexandra was called Felicia. It was of no importance; if they had all changed their name in Braniste, maybe they had changed names in Cimpuletz too; the time could have also come for them, they too could have at least a couple of old women experts in witchcraft.

Jeremy buried his stallion two meters underground in his plum orchard, pulling him there on a sled so as not to have to take him through the whole town to the animal cemetery. That evening he went into the stable, after having whitewashed it in the meanwhile and having gone there with a flyswatter to kill all the flies that could have been infected, and it seemed strange to him that it was quiet and that he heard neither a neigh nor a snort, and only then did he truly understand that the stallion had died, in the darkening solitude of the stable that smelled of slaked lime. And in a way he felt liberated; he didn't have a single care anymore except for one, that of having to buy another horse, and he didn't feel like doing that at all. The doctor and the nurse were riding on the bicycle when he covered the stallion with dirt. And only Bargain and I helped him smooth out the area so that you wouldn't notice that something was buried there; and in the silence with which we stomped the ground that was still moist, about two meters above the dead animal, Jeremy said, as if to himself:

"That one wants to be taken to bed and rolled over on her back, and he lets himself be taken around on her wheels and doesn't understand. She's ripe and wants to get to know what it is that God left to be hers without being hers."

"Yes," said Bargain, and, now sober, he looked at himself below his belt and towards the ground that he was walking on.

"It wants to be." But he didn't say what.

"It would be better if you gave a helping hand."

"Ha, ha," tittered Bargain.

"Women," said Jeremy.

"Right."

"To hell with them; after all, if we're doomed, that's it. Although, he himself has calmed down some; he goes riding on the bicycle. Which is something. He's started taking things easier."

"I don't think it was what she said it was, and isn't."

"What about that one?"

"What one?" asked Bargain.

"The one under us!"

"He might have had something else. Since he's taking things easier and goes riding on the bicycle."

"He's hot for her, if he's riding around."

"But you said he was taking things easier, and not only because of her."

"That's what I'm afraid of, Bargain."

"Why, Jeremy?"

"If Acatrinei isn't struggling anymore and isn't shouting, that doesn't mean things aren't what he said or that it's all over; it's more serious than that; it means that now the great calamity is beginning and that this is the most dangerous moment of the disease, when he himself has gotten tired of yelling about it, he who was so sure! Now he's even more sure, since he doesn't call us to catch curs anymore; he's gotten used to them and to the idea that we can't slaughter them all, and when you get used to insanity, you get used to a truth; it's clear that *it* truly exists, understand? And here's the horror I see: that he's riding around on the bicycle as if it didn't exist, but in fact, in doing this he's showing us once again that the village is full of it, and he's riding around in front of us, but most especially in front of Miss Mia, who doesn't believe, to show us that you can go around too, and not only yell, and that this is another stage of the disease, if yelling doesn't do any good. It's like at cards when somebody bids and somebody else says: I'll take it. Understand? It's a whole new game, but with the same cards; in other words, with the same disease, and he says: I'll take it. But there's no assurance that tomorrow we won't be treated to some new kind of devilry."

"Yes, but why doesn't he take care of what she wants? That would be more humane."

"Maybe he doesn't have the guts."

"But how can she have the guts to go up to any dog?"

"Bargain, that's another kettle of fish: she's not scared of dogs and goes, even at night on her bicycle, through the woods to Cimpuletz or comes back from Turnuvechi, and that's guts, but it's also a kind of challenge. Let's leave aside the dogs. And the highway robbers—who'd want to steal anything from her? But if someone wanted to pull her down off her bicycle, it's not the bicycle he would take, but something you can't steal from someone like her, however much you might want to, and she might even want it to happen and then it's not a question of guts anymore: it's a desire."

"But when she shoots poison into them with an injection, isn't that guts?"

"She's having fun, to use George's expression."

"But when she rides around with him on the bicycle in front of our eyes?"

"She's having fun, first of all; and second, she wants to be for once something other than a girl."

"I get it. But what about him?"

"He's scared of dogs. And even if they weren't rabid he'd be scared of them anyhow. He doesn't have a lot of nerve inside of him, he has what she doesn't: a big heart."

"She doesn't need what he has, don't you hear how she's laughing?"

Miss Mia actually was laughing, and as she pushed down on the pedals, her skirt went up and you could see what can't be seen when you're not riding on a bicycle.

The next day people gathered in Kitchea's backyard, and they were all amazed to see how the chickens there jumped first on one leg, then on the other, cackling and snapping at each other's feathers and anywhere they could catch hold. Since he was a neighbor of Jeremy's, Kitchea said that the cacklers had caught the disease from the stallion buried in the orchard.

"How the hell is that possible, he couldn't have mounted them, since he was tied up?"

"The air," said Kitchea.

"What air?"

"The stallion infected the air, he breathed into it."

At first he laughed—especially because the hens, like creatures deranged by the sun or by drink, were turning around in circles, clucking and knocking each other over, and then snapping with their beaks to peck at flies that seemed to them to exist, but that didn't. Then nobody uttered a word and everybody sniffed the air to see if it had a different smell. Kitchea drove his chickens and chicks into the coop, with the help of some of his neighbors, and when Acatrinei came by to see what was going on there, he saw him catch each chicken under a thick, woolen blanket, take it by the beak and hold it squeezed together until the chicken fell over and was limp and warm and dead in his hands.

"What are you doing?" Acatrinei asked him.

"Keeping the air from getting infected."

"Ah," said Acatrinei, and he didn't show amazement; anyhow, it was hard to be amazed anymore, and even I wasn't amazed. "Go on," he urged him.

"That's what I'm doing. But first I'll make a fire 'cause I forgot."

"Make one."

And Kitchea made a blaze in the backyard with straw and hay. And he brought cornstalks too.

"To burn the air stunk up by that one's stallion."

"Right, right," approved Acatrinei so seriously that I couldn't tell if he had also agreed with the cutting under the tongue, and if I'd be forced to believe, along with everybody else, that he too had gone crazy, just as Kitchea seemed to have gone off his hinges.

"Can you smell it, doctor? The air has a different smell, rabid."

"Who?"

"The air."

"Certainly, certainly, it smells, put more on the fire."

"That's what I'm doing," said Kitchea.

And then he went again with the blanket to catch the chickens and grab them by their beak and kill them by not letting them take any air into their lungs and, above all by not letting them breathe out any diseased air. I don't know where he got the idea that Jeremy's stallion's breath had poisoned the air in his backyard and had infected the poultry. People didn't believe it, but they left with a hand or a handkerchief over their nose anyhow. If rabies had gotten into the air too, and could be carried in the air from house to house, Jeremy was right in saying that a moment had come that was more horrifying than any other so far.

"You were right," Bargain told him, "the sheep will graze on the grass on our heads."

"Kitchea went off his rocker when he saw that guy who gave her the bicycle."

"No, no, my hardness has grown on me again," moaned Bargain.

"Go confess to Margherita."

Bargain left with one hand in his pocket, holding his nose, and with the other blowing out of his nose all the air from Kitchea's backyard.

When the backyard was cleared of people and the only ones left were Acatrinei and the owner of the dead chickens next to the fire, on which I, from up on my stilts, was throwing straw from the top of a stack, for a while all was quiet. Then, all of a sudden, Acatrinei asked:

"How did you know, when you had the candelabra in your arms, that he wanted to throw some people in jail? Not from your own head, not from him; from them, right? And if they told you what he wanted to do, you thought he wasn't the same man you left as boss when they put you behind bars: that he'd been caught. So you admitted what they told you so they'd let you go, which is what they did after you signed. You said 'yes' to what they said, just like to a priest, becaue it never crossed your mind that the man they were talking about with such hatred hadn't been caught in any kind of dangerous act. You thought he'd been locked up and wasn't anymore what he had been, and when they let you go and you found out he was still in the same position as when you left him—the boss—and you'd put your signature to his being a very dangerous character, you got flustered, didn't you?"

"Help me catch the geese too."

"Leave the geese in peace, and quit putting on this show about the air being infected by that one's stallion. Tell me, did you get flustered when they set you free?"

"I was never in jail, doctor. You can ask anybody in the village; not even for one hour. And I don't know what you're talking about."

"But those candelabra that you have in the room where I slept and in the hallway, how long have you had them?"

"I've had them for thirty years, my father won them in a card game with some officers when he was their orderly."

"Yeah, maybe. I see that you've got precise answers, so why are you pretending to burn the air?"

"Who's pretending, me? Smell for yourself, don't you think it has a different stink to it?"

He sniffed the air a number of times and I sniffed it too; it seemed to me that he was right: the smell was muddy with some unknown something, spicy and choking, like a dead mouth of a cat.

The following Thursday Miss Mia came from Cimpuletz really scared. Alexandra, or Felicia, had told her how a cousin of her mother's, after being bitten by a rabid dog and then taken to Turnuvechi for treatment, had still lost her life. When back from the city she had been in the sun, and it's not good to let the sun look upon you; she drank *tzuica* and it's not good to touch any drink; she ate pickles, or was served something to eat and drink, to give her some pleasure and to put her back on her feet, and she didn't get any pleasure, she lay her head on her pillow and passed away. Alexandra or Felicia also said that this had happened when she was little, and the only other thing she remembered now was some cats yowling and scratching and biting and sitting up on top of chimneys or under wood piles like rats, and who struck terror in the children. And she wouldn't have remembered this if they hadn't happened to talk about Kalagherovich (unless it was about another person with the same name) who was bitten by a dog or a cat in some village (she didn't know which), and although the old baba had burned the bite with a poker that was red hot from the blacksmith's bellows, he was now in the hospital in Bucharest, and there wasn't any hope anymore that he'd make it. They took him away from home in an ambulance, and his wife was shocked because he hadn't even shown her the wound, so as not to worry her, and he hadn't even talked to her about what had happened. Rabies was, according to Alexandra (or Felicia), like a kind of phantom that walked around day and night where you least expected it, and it latched onto you anywhere it could and brought you suffering and death, and you had no way of protecting yourself from it because you couldn't tell who had it lying in him (it wasn't only dogs and cats and horses that could have it in their blood), because it went around on tiptoe, silent and deaf and blind as God or the devil had let it travel around the world, uncalled and unwanted, to strike one person or another when you least expected it and had no way of expecting it, if that's how it had been set up by Him above or him below, without the gift of tongue, that is to say, mute and blind. And on the way to Braniste, Mia saw some oxen fallen on the plow land, as wilted as pumpkin plants sweating from the sun beating down on them, with their mouths open, stinking alive of a death that seemed to have entered into them three days before;

and some foxes had cut across the path in front of her bicycle, weak and with their fur pulled out of them, and with their tail between their legs, sleepy. And when Acatrinei laughed at her and at the sleepy foxes she had seen, she got infuriated and asked him why he always thought he was so much smarter than she and than other people about a disease for which there were no experts and better experts, but only non-experts and lesser non-experts, since they couldn't cure it. And she swore that the foxes were sleepy and almost indifferent, so that she could have run over them with her bicycle, and that only one single fox had gotten bewildered when he saw her and had jumped at her, seemingly to bite her, and had even sunk his teeth into the spokes of the back wheel, and the marks could be seen; it was an enraged, crazy fox if after that it started biting its own tail and hind legs until they bled, and howling from pain or helplessness, and pricking up its ears and beating its head in fear, as if trumpets were blaring above it or bells were clanging or hammers were beating on giant metal plates. But the sleepy ones continued on their sleep-filled way, knocking their foreheads against the locust trees (the path went through a locust forest), and then getting up again, indifferent, and continuing on their road that led nowhere; they went wherever they happened to go, sleepy and silent, in search of some solitude and peace. And she saw one scratching the ground under a bush, hiding there in the branches and the sand, skinny and dirty, licking and eating its own filth. And the enraged one, who was a he, continued yelping and biting his tail, and wherever he caught hold, he'd rip his tail, and he tore open with his teeth the balls and belly with which he had produced, or hadn't yet produced, his offspring. And in the woods, farther on, she went over the rotting, repulsive corpses of birds and rabbits. And all over she heard, but didn't see, dogs, or a kind of ghost of dogs barking with cracked or hoarse voices, and creeping along in the grass and the dry, fallen branches, frightening the living rabbits who ran, bumping into each other as if what was chasing them didn't come from only one side, but from all sides at once.

"That's how it might have looked to you," Acatrinei told her. "You were riding in the sun, without a kerchief on your head so your coiffure wouldn't get messed up, and you got a touch of sunstroke."

"Then why didn't I see wolves and boars running to hide from people and from the noise?"

"What noise can there be in the woods?"

"The noise in their heads."

"Then it might have been just a few foxes who had gotten sunstroke and a few scared rabbits."

"Anything else?"

"And the stories you heard at the hairdresser's, and your fear of going through the forest alone."

"Anything else?"

"I don't know."

"No, the foxes were rabid! One of them was howling like a wolf and his mouth was hanging open and he couldn't close it, he couldn't get his jaws together."

"Didn't you maybe dream this last night?"

"No."

"Then maybe you're telling me all this to make fun of me because I believed in rabies and you didn't?"

"No. Come with me into the woods beside the Danube and see."

"I'm not coming."

"Come with me into the woods, what are you afraid of?"

"I'm not afraid of the animals, I'm afraid of you," he laughed.

"What could I do? Oh, why are you thinking such dumb things? What can a girl do to you if you can't do anything to her?"

"Why are you saying dumb things in front of this child?"

"I'm joking."

"I'll come . . ."

"We'll have to take along men with rifles, and maybe their dogs too, so we can eradicate the diseased foxes and rabbits."

"And what are you going to do with the dogs?"

"The dogs will catch the prey more easily, with their sense of smell leading them on."

"Then afterwards won't they get diseased too?"

"No, I'll get the men to shoot them, or I'll give them an injection."

"Leave the dogs and the men in peace. Those men are all spent."

"What do you mean?"

"Okay. Let's go, the two of us, and let's take him too, he'll stay on his stilts and nothing will happen to him if what you say is true. He'll be our witness, to see which of us is lying or dreaming."

"No, I'm not going with a child into a rabid forest. Only with you, if you've got the guts. We'll take Bargain's rifle if you like."

"Okay," he said.

And he went and got the rifle, and the two of them left on the bicycle for the woods on the banks of the Danube.

11

A candelabrum with six lighted, sputtering, tallow candles, attracting around it a dance of black, lively flies,
making no noise with their wings, just floating in a frag-
mented dance up and down and to one side and the other,
and under the candeladrum, lying on a blanket of fine
wool with little rose buds on the edges and peacocks looking eye to eye at each other, was a shaggy, giant, fero-
cious, three-headed dog, barking in turn with each of his
three mouths, like a puppy, a bitch, and a mastiff, all of a
sudden when the flies, innocent in their innocence,
would sit on its tail or forehead. It was as if I was dreaming and didn't want to wake up so that I could watch
attentively that prodigy with the three muzzles, which I
thought I had seen somewhere before, or had met sometime before, really or maybe only in sleep. Pecker appeared too, in the bridegroom's suit, and Alexandra's (Felicia's) cousin, and those who had been chanted to nasally
in a priestly way by Evangeline came to see the six eyes of
the beast, and it started barking at them deafeningly, and
they laughed and didn't get at all frightened, and to me it
seemed normal for the dead to laugh once they had left for
another part of the world, but I didn't understand how
they'd lost their fear of people. I woke up, I think, and
then went back to sleep immediately and continued
seeing everything I'd seen; the flies had, however, multiplied, and the candelabrum had become seven candelabra,
and the dead had become seventy-seven, in groups of ten
or so, each group under six lighted candles. Only the dog
still had three heads, and barked with three tongues and,
seemingly in three languages, and it tried in vain to scare
the people in front of it; it couldn't do them any harm—

they were dead—but it was clear that it couldn't do them any good either. Then the heads started eating the peacocks on the fine wool blanket, and the roses, and the flies from the air, and they started swallowing the candelabra with all the lighted candles. And I don't know what happened: did they also swallow Pecker in the bridegroom's suit and the others, or did they all disappear into the darkness that was left after the candles perished? In the morning I told my dream to George and he didn't give me any solution; he burped and showed me Miss Mia who was washing at Sofronie's well, ever watched by Bargain from the shed where he was hidden in the corncobs. Then she sat down on a chair and washed her feet in a basin, and her knees, illuminated by the soft, morning light made me think back to Acatrinei and I seemed to see him again seated in front of them, gazing at them and washing them (as he had also gazed at them and washed them in the Danube after they had come out of the woods in the evening), and once again, gazing at them and washing them with water and wet sand. Bargain had no peace, like a starved rat among ears of corn without any corn on them, and I'm sure that he too was gazing at the same thing I was looking at with George, but crazed with a desire that he didn't have the courage to fulfill and that he didn't even dream of fulfilling, or didn't know how to yet.

And George said: "She looks at them like at two altars."

And I answered him and George jabbed at the side of the shed with a splinter and said: "Siss!"—as if to a bird that might have been there. "Now a gaze right into the altar," said George and he laughed in my face with his rotten, stinking teeth, and drank his portion of morning *tzuica* and left.

The air behind him remained full of stench, or so it seemed to me, because that stench stayed in my nose and didn't leave me the whole day; because, afterwards when I saw those two dead gypsies next to the stream, I didn't smell anything unusual in the air. Those two weren't among the ones who had eaten Bargain's cow, they were some others. We had a number of them in the village, and up to then a number had died, but nobody had paid any attention, and now something unimaginable had happened: dead gypsies were noticed because it was supposed that they kicked the bucket, diseased. Thus it wasn't enough for them to die in order to have the village gather around them, they also had to be rabid, or presumed so. People drew near, but still kept their distance to look at them; no one dared to go up beside them, as if they might get up from the dead and bite them and fill them with slobber and hoarseness too. There was no longer any God if even their family didn't put a black handkerchief over their eyes, or an apron, so that the flies wouldn't settle on them, in their eyes, and eat into them with their diligence. Eventually everybody found out that they were the Assholer brothers, and that their father and mother had died a couple of weeks before, shut up in their house: death had followed death, mother after father, five days apart; and after they had been buried, those twin brothers didn't sleep in the house anymore, they ate with neighbors, and four days before, they had set fire to the house that seemed to them to be guilty, with its doors and windows, with its thatched roof and its brick hearth, guilty with the place on which it stood, and cursed. So they burned it down to its foundations and they didn't let anyone bring so much as a bucket of water to throw on the fire. And they also poured gasoline on the fence that surrounded the house and set a match to its base, and they burned up the plum trees as well, the only two they had, and the walnut tree (with gasoline all over), and the ground (doused all over with gasoline) in the front yard so that misfortune wouldn't go from them to other people— and indeed, it didn't go to other people, it came down on their heads once again, despite the fact that they slept in strawstacks in the fields. The curse was contagious, whispered the women when they saw that no one would go near those two lying beside the stream. They were stretched out, one right beside the other, as if they had lain down to sleep, and instead of being "caught" by sleep for the night, they were "caught" by sleep forever. Berlinbei (the one who burned Bargain's cow's head) said that old Assholer could tell when a fit was coming on him, and would tell his family: "Come and tie me up, and get out of here and don't come near me until I calm down." And they would tie him up with a rope by the walnut tree (he was on a chair for a while, and later was just on straw), and then the evil would seize him, just as he had foreseen, and make him foam at the mouth and twist about, and everybody thought it was falling sickness, since he was aware of its coming on him and since, after it passed, he always recognized them and called them by name and went about his affairs: he made sandals and pounded soles on boots (he was a shoemaker). And when, after that kind of fit, he went back to normal and was dead, they still believed it was falling sickness. But old lady Assholer, when she saw him laid out, had an inkling of what kind of death had struck him down (all deaths were the same to her if he didn't exist anymore), and she started to hiccough; for two days she hiccoughed, until they put him under the grass. After that she got a fever in her joints, where you get rheumatism, and the fever rose to her head; and in the night she writhed about and woke up saying that snakes were eating her, and that they had gone into her belly when she drank milk and grew in her, sucking all her flesh, and she would die if she didn't poison them or puke them out. She would die when the snakes no longer had anything left to gnaw in her; they would appear one day in her place, and one day she would be no more. That's what she dreamed, and all day long she scratched her belly and her back; she said it felt like pins and needles, that the snakes had had babies and when they mated to have more babies, they made her itch inside with their tongues and their tails. And in addition to the hiccoughs she got the sneezes, and those boys of hers spent the whole day saying: "God bless you, God bless you!" And see what a blessing she got from that sneeze-hiccoughing: she went after her old man. She died quietly, not like somebody rabid; sneezing. Her heart had broken inside her when she saw Assholer not moving anymore; and I think that at that moment she got rabid too, because of a broken heart, if she really did die of rabies. But, what put the fear of the devil in those two and made them set fire to the house wasn't her death (the old man had died and in that suffering there was still room for more, that she would pass away too), their fright was such that, not knowing where the evil on their house came from, they set fire to the house and the land, and this fright came especially from her sneeze when she breathed her last breath.

"God bless you, God bless you," the two of them said to her, and when they looked more closely, they didn't have anyone to talk to anymore.

"Man, look at this," they said, and didn't want to believe it, and put their hands on her; she was warm.

And she stayed warm still when they rubbed her with vinegar, warm, as if alive, but without breath or heartbeat.

"How the goddamn hell can anybody live without breathing, and with a silent heart," they asked themselves and each other and us who had come to their house.

But the old lady had truly died; and the fever hadn't left her, not even after two days. She started to smell really like the dead when they put her next to her old man; and still the flesh on her was warm. It might have been because of summer, I don't know. They thought it was a curse, or that the snakes were still alive in her. They too had fallen into childishness, if they chased after dreams.

"And look at them now, so peaceful; they don't have a care in the world anymore," said Berlinbei, the one who ate Bargain's cow.

And when Acatrinei came with Miss Mia, everybody was still talking, making big plans to do this and that, but they weren't doing anything: not even the dead can be buried with words alone.

"Why don't you pick them up and take them into a backyard?" the nurse asked them.

And again Berlinbei found an answer that took them off the hook: that they had been waiting for them, and were waiting also for someone from the district attorney's office to look at the dead people and determine that they weren't poisoned by somebody, or hadn't poisoned themselves.

"That's dumb, they died of rabies," said Miss Mia, strongly convinced. "Come and get them."

But still nobody went near the Assholer brothers, and Acatrinei whispered to her: "I told you they were spent."

And only when George arrived too did they wrap the dead men in a blanket and take them on a sled into their burned front yard. And on the road, dragging the sled in the sand, harnessed to it with Acatrinei, George asked him too:

"What do you mean by spent?"

"You can't expect anything from them."

"Yes, I get it," said George.

I didn't get it until he told me in the Assholer yard what he had understood: "Like money that you have and then don't have anymore, they've been spent."

"And?"

"And they're not whole men, they're like shadows that you can't expect anything of."

"I see, and who spent them?"

"They did, or those they lived under, the war, town hall, the land, the non land, those above them."

"Yes," I said, but still I didn't understand at that time. Then Bargain appeared with one hand in his pocket and a lighted candle in the other; he was coming with it from church where he had been to pray for his folks and himself, and he came praying all along the road as well, saying after each Pater Noster (the only prayer he knew), "Lord, forgive me." So that the candle was taken from him by George and put at the head of the two brothers who were laid out in the shade of the walnut tree, burned and black as a scarecrow. Bargain took another candle from his pocket and continued his prayer while lighting it.

"There's nothing wrong with you," Acatrinei told him, blowing out his candle.

Bargain got incensed and lit the candle again and told him:

"What about Jeremy's stallion? 'Cause I haven't gotten over this yet."

"It's something else."

"What?"

"Priapism."

"What's that?"

"It doesn't come from what you think."

"But what if it does? If you're tricking me, what can I do to you?"

"Nothing. It's not it, you don't have the symptoms. And there isn't even any rabies in the village."

"Oh yes there is, don't lie anymore," Miss Mia put in.

And what seemed strange to me was not only her harsh voice, or that she didn't agree with him, but that his opinion didn't even count anymore, wasn't of interest to her anymore. She didn't even look at him, and kept arranging with the women about making funeral bread for the dead, and with the men about making a place for them next to the old Assholers (they had a name totally unsuited to such a death, or maybe it was suited to its idiocy).

"It won't even be hard, the ground still hasn't packed down there over them, so we can heap it up over all four of them, to be a kind of monument, beautiful," said Berlinbei.

And that's just the way it was done the next day; they put the same earth over all four and decorated it with flowers, and it was just as Berlinbei had said: beautiful.

"If they could see this they'd be delighted," said

Berlinbei. "They can be happy now, they never dreamed of such a monument and such a big cross. It's beautiful, that's what it is, just beautiful."

But Miss Mia didn't behave any differently with Acatrinei: I mean, she behaved exactly as (or maybe even more stupidly than) she had behaved before going on the bicycle into the locust forest next to the banks of the Danube. And I'm the only one who saw them when they came out of the woods, how they washed each other in the water, so full of each other, and how he washed her knees, and not only her knees. From up on stilts, in the leaves and branches of a poplar where I was waiting for them, I saw them. And she seemed to have forgotten, and even the next day after that she behaved as if there hadn't been anything between them. I don't know if they found the foxes and rabbits and birds she talked about; but it was certain—at least I was certain of it—that the two of them went into the Danube as naked as light. And at least for that reason I thought she should have spoken to him differently. Toward afternoon and evening, when they were going home to eat or sleep, he kept asking her:

"When will we see each other again?"

And his words had silliness in them too. After all, they were going to stay in the village and had to meet up with each other that same day or the next. But as for her, there wasn't even any silliness in her behavior. She didn't shake hands with him in parting, and didn't tell him either that they should meet again sometime, although she'd really liked it all back there at the Danube. And he was even more ridiculous: in the evening I saw him knocking on her door and bringing her a bunch of roses (I think he stole them from the school yard). And she didn't say anything one way or another, she put them in a basin of water and set them outside the door and said:

"Flowers aren't good to have in the house at night."

And he laughed and didn't stay (also, the owner of the house, Sofronie, came back from the fields). And in the morning I saw how the roses had been pecked by the hens. And I asked myself why he hadn't stolen the roses from the school before going to the Danube with her, and why he shouted at her back then and fought with her, and now that they had, in any case, washed each other in the water (that I was sure of), his voice trembled when he was with her.

"Why?" I asked George.

"I don't know, maybe that's city style."

"Style or no style with the stealing, but with his words? Why now (because I heard him) did he say: 'Miss, I . . . how can I say it?'—Why now?"

"That's easy. Because he's head-over-heels."

"And what about her, why isn't she like him?"

"She's more devilish; she wants him to boil. Or she wants to be free, still free."

"But what about at the Danube?"

"Hogwash," George told me, "you dreamed you saw them in the Danube. Maybe that's the way you wanted to see them."

"I didn't dream it."

"But what if you did dream it?"

12

Bargain started going around drunk all the time with a lighted candle in his hand, and although there was no connection between *tzuica* and the "Pater Noster" he recited almost uninterruptedly, he never parted company from the bottle or the prayer, saying that these were the only things left to him after he gave up his house, like the Assholer brothers, and that soon he'd be left with nothing, just like them. He lay down to sleep wherever he happened to be, and he lost all sense of shame; he mated with Margherita by the side of the road, morning or afternoon, and they didn't care about who might be passing by on their way to the fields, or riding home, and they didn't give a damn if children or old women walked by near them. Margherita had no way of knowing what shame was; she was, as George said, like a sheep or a crow or a hen. But Bargain had gone off his rocker and expected to be taken off by people at any moment and be put into a chicken coop, like poor Pecker, and he even shouted at Acatrinei, and cursed him and asked him why he didn't tie him up, and why he didn't get Miss Mia to give him an injection. And the doctor told him not to drink anymore if he wanted him to believe he was sick, and not to ask anymore to be tied up, because so long as he was guzzling *tzuica* and wine, it showed that maybe the very disease he was afraid of couldn't do anything against such drinking. Bargain wouldn't let himself be taken care of either by Jeremy with whom he was friends, or George, or the brothers with such different names, not by anybody. He wouldn't take food or clean shirts so as not to repeat the experience of the Assholer brothers who, the more their people took care of them and were close to them, the shorter their road to the grave was.

"Don't come near me, because the closer you are to me the closer you are to death," said he.

And Acatrinei laughed in his face and told him to put down the bottle and take a break and eat and sleep in a bed like a human being and not in the straw like the animals, so that tuberculosis wouldn't by some chance strike him down. And perhaps it was out of anger at Acatrinei, because he didn't take him seriously, that Bargain acted like a fool in front of everybody, and nothing mattered to him anymore and he no longer had any shame and said dirty things all the time and got all full of sand with Margherita wherever he happened to meet up with her, and one day walked over to the church naked, and went up to the altar and barked at the saints and then wept and lit all the candles in the candle holders and prayed on his knees with his hands together in front of him and kissed all the icons, but then seeing that the sign that gave him the assurance that he was sick didn't change and didn't fade, and no spirit came down to soften his hardness, he barked again at the saints and went to get the rope from the church bell to put around his neck and kill himself, and he couldn't do it at first because he was too short to reach it; and then, having reached it and tied it around his neck, he couldn't die because the bell was big and tipped down on one side when it was pulled by the rope, and the rope didn't actually get longer, or rather it did in the sense that, when it was pulled down, it changed its length by the amount corresponding to the distance between the stationary position of the bell and its position when it was pulled downward to about its maximum, and that distance, which the rope appeared to lengthen, made Bargain's feet touch the ground, and the clapper bounced him like a ball since he was so small, and it rang and brought people into the church and they found him in that ridiculous position and took him away, and his friend Jeremy said:

"What's with you, dummo; you're so scared of what would happen if rabies got into you that you've lost your mind and want to hang yourself?"

And when they took him to the clinic, wrapped in a blanket from head to toe, as if in a sack, almost tied up in it, Acatrinei didn't send him to the hospital, nor did he even lock him up in a room alone, he sent him home and told him to quit it because there wasn't a damn thing wrong with him.

"Hasn't his personality changed?" asked Miss Mia.

"His personality hasn't changed at all, what do you see changed in him?"

"He's wilder."

"Who knows why that might be."

"It's changed," said Bargain.

"What?"

"The what-do-you-call-it."

"Your personality?"

"Yes, my personality. Isn't this a part of a personality?" he said, and threw the blanket off his shoulders.

And then they all saw him the way the saints in church had seen him too. Miss Mia went into the clinic and George poured the jug of water from the table over him.

"Calm down, you!"

And Bargain licked the water that had dropped on his lips.

"Nothing wrong with you if even this morning I saw you getting up out of Sofronie's corncobs. I know what you want."

"What do I want?"

"I know but I don't want to tell!"

"But I wanted to kill myself."

That was right and nobody had an answer for it, and Bargain left, pulling the blanket up from the ground onto his back and wrapping himself up in it like a shroud. And Acatrinei said something about taste, that his hadn't changed and that he wasn't doing what people afflicted with the virus usually do, and that one could talk to him, and I think he said that Bargain didn't have a perverted sense of taste to want to swallow stones or money or other things. So George ran after Bargain and brought him back by the arm and blew on him with the air from his stinking mouth and fanned him with the blanket and gave him a jug of water to drink and told him:

"There's nothing wrong with you, you don't mind water or air blowing on you, what you care about are the legs of I know who; they made you bark!" and he gave him a kick in the lower part of a man's backside and shoved him out onto the road.

Sofronie started to tell how, around Calafat where he had been at an aunt's house, the heat and the drought had brought rabies into the village, and there, not like in Braniste, all the men had taken their dogs, all tied up, into the school yard and had killed them with fence posts in front of each other (without their being all diseased, or maybe not a single one of them was afflicted), and then two professional dogcatchers from Turnuvechi had skinned them, and with the skins they had bought rugs for the town hall and the school, and what was left after the dogs were flayed, they buried on the outskirts of the village in a lime kiln; however, they didn't put dirt over the dead bodies that no longer had any color or name (skinned, all dogs looked alike, and it amazed their masters that they didn't recognize them anymore), until after they had poured gasoline on them and set them on fire (the fat on them sizzled as it burned).

"Those rugs will bark and bite people's feet," said George.

"One guy hid his dog, he didn't want to kill him, and the cur bit him and the man died barking."

"Hogwash," said Acatrinei.

"No, I saw his cross for myself. Rabies started there one day out of the blue, because it's a village surrounded by water, on an island in the Danube, and no outside dogs have set foot in it for years, and even people from other villages don't go there, except by boat three times a year, Easter, Whitsundtide, and Assumption Day."

"That's why I don't believe it. This epidemic falls from the heavens everywhere, or appears all of a sudden, the way you said; I simply don't believe it. Rabies doesn't come, if it comes, without coming from somewhere."

"But where does it come from?"

"Even I don't know for sure. From dogs, first of all."

"And where do they get it?" George was interested.

"I don't know exactly."

"You see, it still has to come from somewhere, from the heat, from thirst, from the air, from the ground," said Sofronie.

"From the air," was Kitchea's view of it.

"You'd do well to shut up," Acatrinei told him.

"Okay, I'll shut up," said Kitchea, and he left, but at the gate he asked:

"Why should I shut up?"

"So that you don't beat the air with your mouth!"

"Okay."

"Miss, let me borrow your bicycle," said Acatrinei.

"You're going off again?"

"Again."

"No point."

"That's not what I think."

And Acatrinei left on the bicycle and only when he was out of sight did I learn from others' talk that he left for the Cimpuletz hospital to look for Kalagherovich and to get him out of there, out of the hands of dummos who had never seen rabies in their life, and who might kill him, hale and hearty, with medication claiming they were trying to make him well. He had been there before and hadn't found him, and in the evening when he returned, he was down at the mouth; he hadn't come across him either at the hospital in Turnuvechi, where he managed to get to on a truck. He only found that he had been in the insane asylum several days earlier, and had tried to cut his throat with a piece of tin but hadn't succeeded: they saved him. Acatrinei felt it was strange that no one had even seen him there, but everyone said he had gone off in an ambulance, and after his desperate attempt, had gone off again in the ambulance, no one knew where, to another hospital most likely. There wasn't a single sheet of paper that had his name recorded on it. Finally, he heard that he was still in Cimpuletz, isolated in a room in a former boyard mansion that had been turned into a tuberculosis sanatorium.

"But what do you have to do with him, he's not your brother?" Jeremy asked.

"Nothing, but I'd like to see if he is or isn't sick; and if he is, then he left here sick—when he came and gave Miss Mia the bicycle he was in good health—but if he's not, it's even worse, and still it's from here, I think, from Braniste, that the disease comes which they say he has. And it seems horrible to me, Jeremy, to make a man die for a disease he doesn't have."

And every day for a week he went to Cimpuletz for nothing, and the school principal, who came through Braniste in his buggy from Patirlagele, finding that he was still going around here and there every day on the bicycle, said that maybe the doctor too had been bitten by a dog because he had no peace, or maybe, he laughed, he had found somebody and was going to meet her and was telling lies about looking for Kalagherovich.

"In any case, Kalagherovich isn't sick, who came up with that lie?"

And he went off in his buggy, and in the evening when Kitchea told Acatrinei what the principal had said, he didn't answer anything. It was only the next morning that he asked me to tell Kitchea to come to the clinic, and he asked him:

"How are your chickens doing?"

"I killed them all."

"And the geese?"

"Them too."

"And Kalagherovich?"

"What about him?"

"Didn't you kill him too?"

"How would I kill him?"

"With a blanket over his head, so he couldn't get any air."

"God forbid," said Kitchea, and when he passed by Miss Mia he told her what he had talked about with the doctor and added: "He's not normal. The principal was right."

"What did the principal say?"

"What the others heard too."

"What?" insisted Miss Mia.

"I don't know, I forgot."

"Did you find Kalagherovich?" Miss Mia asked Acatrinei.

"No."

"Don't even look for him anymore. Maybe it wasn't even he who was here, or maybe he doesn't even exist, but if he exists and was here, you may never even find him."

"I have to look for him."

"You're better off staying in the village; I don't even go to Cimpuletz anymore on Thursdays. The sheep have gotten rabid in Braniste."

"I have to go; I told the men here what to do, and they didn't all do it if you say now it's the sheep's turn."

"Stay, convince them to kill the sheep."

"I have to find Kalagherovich before it's too late."

"Maybe they took him to Bucharest."

"I'll go even there."

"Or somewhere else."

"I'll find his trail."

"And the sheep?"

"To hell with the sheep, you take care of them, you know what to do to them."

"Okay," said Miss Mia.

And she went to Jeremy in the kitchen and asked him

what the principal from Patirlagele had said. Early the next morning the doctor left again for Cimpuletz on the bicycle while Miss Mia, surrounded by Zabic, Bargain (who forgot what was the matter with him when she sent word that she needed him), Jeremy, Kitchea, the brothers with such different names, and others went from gate to gate and looked at each sheep one by one. There were some who had lost their wool like rags; others were so weak they didn't even know how to bleat anymore. They no longer sent them out in the field, out of fear of the dogs, and now their skin hung from their bodies. And because of hunger or illness, they didn't make it to the water buckets that were put out in front of them, or to the troughs full of water. And that was "Pecker's symptom," as they said in Braniste; to die of thirst before you actually died. Or even better, in George's lingo: first of all to have your blood go cold, and after that to have your thirst die in you; that is to say, your thirst wouldn't die in you before your heart died. And they slaughtered the sheep in the sheepfolds so as not to bury them alive, and they burned them on piles of dry branches, and nobody wept over them. The children had been shut up in their houses with the doors padlocked so they wouldn't see, but more especially so that some crazed sheep wouldn't brand them with its diseased eyes (there wasn't any fear of their biting), since you could, said the old women, get the disease through the eyes. There wasn't enough room to bury them or burn them in the animal cemetery on the outskirts of the village, so they dug graves in every garden, and every garden became a cemetery.

And they all dug in the ground in an unbelievable frenzy, and waited for Miss Mia to put a mirror in front of each sheep's eyes to see if it would shy away from it and get the shakes from seeing itself in a mirror, which is what happened to Pecker, according to Baba Sevastitza. And so, either the sheep would see themselves and be amazed at their own sight, or the reflected light from the mirror would blind them, or it would be a symptom of the disease if they ran away and bleated after seeing their own eyes in a mirror—all, or almost all of them would then have to be slaughtered and skinned. But the people, almost without exception, didn't need any more skins or wool; so they burned them just as they were and the whole village smelled of suet, as if tallow candles had been lighted all over the place and everyone and everything was in a church, immense and invisible, but still a church if the air smelled of lighted candles.

At Sofronie's they used up the wood and then emptied the corncob shed and put cornstalks and dried dung on the fire too, just to make a big blaze. Sofronie wanted to have all the sheep and all the disease perish at once and to have his backyard sparkle. And he lent out some corncobs too, and his sheep and those of the other people died in front of their eyes, and nobody shed a tear, just as nobody had mourned the death of the Assholer brothers. And they remembered the Assholer brothers who had been put next to their old folks without even a sigh, and they thought about how they were people too, and how they couldn't sleep in the ground if unmourned, and how their souls were now wandering through the village, diseased, and maybe carrying the disease from door to door. The dogs who were still alive were tied up. And so that the Assholer brothers could sleep in peace, the women went and censed their grave and wept for them beside their cross. And then everybody wept over his own sheep, because they were souls too and they too could wander, unlamented, through the village carrying the horrible epidemic. White, like corpses, the sheep waited to die without rotting, to be burned, and listened silently to the weeping of Sofronie or Zabic or someone else, and they didn't realize, of course, that they put tears in their eyes with spit, from their fingers, and that they mourned, winking and screwing up their eyes at each other, the sheep just thought it was crying.

And after they finished with the sheep, Miss Mia told them to eat a good meal and have a drink and come to the clinic and then go out with their rifles and dogs into the forest near the Danube, to burn everything there that was full of worms and hunt everything that was afflicted with disease, to clean out the area and leave the forest as virgin as before. And to take the dogs with them, on leash, to smell out the prey, and when it wasn't possible to catch a fox or a rabbit just by going along with the dogs, then to unleash them, and any of the dogs who caught the quarry either in his mouth or with his claws, or even if he only touched it, was to be killed too, on the spot so as to stamp out the very seed of the epidemic. That day I didn't go to the forest with them and didn't see Acatrinei meet up with them and quarrel with them, as I heard them doing the next morning when I was in the forest with sleep still in my eyes, up in a poplar tree right on the riverbank, and they passed noisely by with their dogs on leash. Miss Mia said they should meet at about noon, around the place where the Saturday River flows into the Danube, and they should be careful not to be fooled when they saw foxes dragging their hind legs as they did yesterday, silent ones; they too were rabid and should be burned close to the Danube so that the forest wouldn't catch fire. She told Bargain to stay with her so that together they could beat down the banks of the Saturday River where, in other times, wolves had come to satisfy their thirst. Everybody left, and all day long I heard rifles boom and I saw the leaves tremble from the booming, and I could see the path leading to Cimpuletz, white in the grasses on the banks of the Danube, the forest clearing, and the sand around the Saturday River, and beyond the locust forest I could see and did see the smoke of their blazing fires. Bargain came back drunk (but Miss Mia had taken the rifle from him so that he wouldn't do anything stupid), and he was singing, scaring the birds, and his joyfulness made him look like somebody who was just getting over an illness that he was still convinced he had. Zabic and Sofronie, and the brothers with such different names, and Kitchea, and Jeremy were impatient and frightened, and only then did I understand what George meant when he said about them: "They're electrified." Some people in Turnuvechi were trying to get electricity brought to the mill, the school and the church, and this was said to be "electrification;" but I hadn't heard anybody except George say that people could be electrified too. However, in his opinion they were, because rabies had come into the village and into everybody, if not as the disease then as the terror of that disease, each of them with his own form of it, each one frightened of what the other people had, whether it was the disease or the other people's terror of the disease; in other words, electrified—wanting to escape at any price and ready to do anything they could to escape, burning like the light bulbs in the shape of candles in the church, or set in motion like the mill saw or its roller. The dogs too, starved so that they wouldn't become rabid, finding themselves in the forest and knowing why, because they had been brought there before to hunt, trembled with impatience, their nostrils flared and their ears pricked to the slightest ripple of the air, their eyes grown more savage and keener. Now as they barked, stirring up the forest, it was like a wedding for them, or like their hour of mating. As I was listening to them I saw Miss Mia coming alone and naked into the Danube. She had torn herself away from Bargain; maybe she had sent him off after the others. She paddled around in the water and then came out to lie down on the hot sand of the riverbank, and the yapping of the dogs didn't bother her in the least, and I think she didn't even notice that, in this hour of the dogs, calm had totally disappeared from everywhere, because around her there was peace and quiet and the sun was beating hotly on her breasts and lower down, making her drowsy. She moved more into the shade but left her feet in the sun and fell asleep, or dozed off; she stayed there without moving for a long time, then went over to the food basket that was still in the woods on a tree branch, where her clothes were too, and she came back after almost an hour eating apples, and waded into the Danube, and ate apples there too. And once again she stretched out on the sand and only then did I notice the bicycle that had belonged to Kalagherovich leaning against a locust tree, and when I looked more carefully I could also make out Acatrinei. If he had been with her I wouldn't have been surprised; I wouldn't have been surprised either at his not getting into the Danube with her—so that the hunters wouldn't by some chance catch sight of them. But that's not the way it was; Acatrinei was dressed and his shirt was wet on his back and he stared at her without taking his hands off the handlebars, and that meant he had just gotten there from Cimpuletz. And when she went again to the place where she had left her clothes and he appeared in front of her, I couldn't see his face, only hers; she got scared and started to scream. And I laughed to myself, and laughed too when he took off after her and they disappeared in the direction of the place where her clothes must have been and she kept on screaming. The hunters were far away. She came toward the riverbank shouting and holding her clothes in her arms, and trying to get dressed, and not being able to in the haste that gripped her; but I didn't detect any excitement in her voice, and, in fact, I wasn't interested in her screaming; she was naked, so now George couldn't tell me ever again that I was dreaming she was like that on the banks of the Danube. And if she was screaming, that was an even surer sign that she was alive and wasn't a dream of mine. Acatrinei came after her infuriated, but she didn't wait for him to get close and ran again toward that place I couldn't see at all from the poplar. Maybe she had gotten angry because he'd seen her like that, or maybe he said something to her, or maybe she didn't want to see him anymore because she thought that he was coming from some woman in Cimpuletz. It seemed to be his fault for coming and seeing her, unexpectedly and uncalled, but despite the fact that she was screaming and that her eyes were burning with fury, those eyes were more stunning like that and her fury made her even more beautiful, and

that's why I could only laugh and wait for her to calm
down and take him by the hands and lead him over to the
Danube, as she did the other time I saw them, or when I
dreamed I saw them; or not to calm down and, unap-
peased and spiteful, to take him by the hands and go to
that same place in the Danube. But she disappeared again
in the thick of the locusts and I heard a shot and it startled
me. But it was nothing. Acatrinei came along the bank
alone; she hadn't shot at him. But he was still angry and
he had, I thought, good reason to be: the game was lasting
too long, or her anger was lasting too long, and it was
beginning to look real. And it was real because, enraged,
he shouted something in her direction. They quarrelled
without my being able to see them or hear what they
were really saying to each other. And then I saw Bargain
coming toward the bank of the Danube too. He had heard
the gunshot and was the first to come, I thought. Nothing
more would happen now; those two couldn't go into the
Danube together anymore. You could hear the dogs ap-
proaching also, barking. Acatrinei lowered his voice and
followed her near the Danube, begging her for something
and trying to explain something to her; in vain, for she,
who had gotten dressed, ran away from him, still barefooted and trying to tuck her dishevelled hair under her
scarf. So he sat down, with his face in his hands, on a
bleached out willow tree trunk that had been brought up
on the bank by the waves, and she moved away from him
with Bargain and stayed a distance away from him until
all the others who had left before came back, and they
looked at him, they and their barking, leashed dogs. And
he looked at her and at them and, reaching out his hand
toward her and toward them and motioning them to
come near him, said: "Miss . . ."

But nobody answered, and then I understood that his
anger came from his discovery: that she could stand not
being near him and could even live without him, which
was exactly what she wanted, and therefore he was alone
just as he was then, sitting on the willow that had been

bleached and rotted by the water, and being alone meant that he was not indispensable to her, and the fact that she didn't feel his absence was worse than, or at least as bad as, loneliness; he no longer had any purpose. I often thought afterwards about the moments he spent sitting there on the willow, and I'm convinced even now that, sitting there, he learned what jealousy is; I repeat, jealousy, because he was unable to think of anything else. Jealousy, that fear of his that he would stay there alone on the banks of the Danube and she would go to the village and never even say goodby to him; that was the danger he felt; loneliness, that is to say, exactly what, in essence, jealousy is. He laughed, however, and told Miss Mia:

"Quit joking! . . ."

"He's rabid," I heard her say.

"Why are you saying dumb things?"

"He came after me to bite me."

"I came after you like any other man and I scared you because I found you with . . ."

"He's delirious. His eyes are red, look at him!"

"I haven't slept . . ."

"He told me . . . Oh how he told me! The things he told me! And the way he ran after me to tear me to pieces . . . He's delirious . . . He won't touch water . . . Come on, get into the Danube and drink water!"

He didn't answer, he just sat there with his face in his hands.

"He has a headache, like Pecker."

"Let's catch him and tie him up."

"And what if he bites or scratches us?"

"Let's leave him here."

"What if he comes into the village and bites some child?"

"Let's catch him and tie his hands."

"Would you go near him?"

"Quit joking," he told them, "go mind your own business."

The whole forest smelled of burned flesh and the fires were smoking on the banks.

"Kalagherovich is alive."

"He's delirious . . ."

"Quit joking," he said and stood up and went toward them.

But only the dogs stayed where they were, barking; they and she took a step back.

"Stay where you are," shouted Kitchea.

"You sold out Kalagherovich . . ."

"He's delirious, I didn't even know him," said Kitchea.

"Here, drink some water from this canteen," Sofronie threw him a military canteen.

Acatrinei gave it a kick and it flew into the Danube.

"He doesn't want any . . ."

"Go take a bath," Jeremy told him. "Pull off your clothes and get into the water naked to see if you're not afraid of it."

Acatrinei laughed and went toward them, but in fact stayed the same distance away because with each step he took toward them, they took a step back.

"Come on, get into the Danube."

"Aren't you ashamed of yourselves, you idiots?"

"He called us idiots," said Kitchea and threw down a cudgel that he had in his hand.

"What do you want, me to take it in my teeth and show that I'm what you want me to be? Here you are, I'm taking it," he said, and he took the piece of wood in his mouth angrily and then threw it in Kitchea's direction and started to laugh. "Come on, enough of this game, let's go home," he added.

"Get into the Danube . . ."

"Get done with this game, for God's sake, you're not funny . . ."

"Drink some water . . ."

"His eyes are red."

"I'm leaving you, I'm going back to the village alone,"

he said, and he went to get his bike. But long before, Bargain had taken it away from where he had left it. "Miss, tell them to give me back my bike . . ."

"He's staggering around."

"He's turning around in place . . ."

"I'm looking for my bike . . .Come on, for God's sake, I've had enough. Tomorrow I have to go see Kalagherovich."

"He's delirious . . ."

"Look at him, he fell on his face . . ."

"A tree stump in the grass. I'm tired, I want to go home and get some sleep. I'm not in the mood for bad jokes . . ."

"Tie yourself up with this rope," Kitchea threw him a rope taken from an army pack that had become a hunting bag.

Acatrinei threw it into the Danube and didn't answer. She put a mirror in front of his eyes and Acatrinei turned away and smiled sadly.

"I don't like your childish pranks, playing with a mirror after everything I saw . . ."

"What did you see?" asked Sofronie.

"He's delirious and he can't stand the mirror. These are sure signs . . ."

"How dumb can you get? . . . As dumb as your chase through the woods after rabbits . . . You look like fools with your rifles and your curs . . . Come on, beat it," he said, and he sat down again on the willow with his face in his hands.

Kitchea had another rope in his bag; he took it out and motioned for somebody to come up to Acatrinei on the sly and tie him up. Nobody wanted to and in the frenzied pandemonium of the dogs I didn't hear what they told each other in whispers. One of them had a dog get loose from him, leash and all, and that mastiff went up to Acatrinei barking. Acatrinei picked up a piece of the willow to defend himself and hit the dog on the head and flipped him over on his back. The dog writhed and then rushed at him even more furiously, yelping, and he hit him again and knocked him down in the sand, but it was clear from his cursing that fear had come upon him with greater force than the dog.

"Call off your beast," he shouted.

But nobody uttered a word. They watched how he fought with the dog and how he hit it clumsily. He went over to a locust and wanted to climb up in it and escape from the persistence of the injured cur; he didn't climb up, maybe out of shame.

"Tell them to call off their cur," he shouted.

Nobody answered.

"You're really conceited, horribly vicious . . . is this how you're going to get your revenge, making me the butt of your joke in this idiotic game?"

He was circling around the locust, using sand and his jacket to fight off the cur who was spurred on by the barking of the others on leash.

"Well, I'll have to admit that you're right, you're more of an expert in all diseases than I, and I won't take any patients away from you the way you think, the ones you give injections to for the price of eggs and chickens so that you can go the hairdresser in Cimpuletz . . . Come on, don't make me turn mean too . . . Why are you so proud of being listened to by a bunch of . . . Make eyes at that midget too . . . Go with whomever you want, wherever you want, I won't ever again . . ."

"He's delirious, do you hear him?"

"What the Goddamn hell did I ever do to make you so angry that you won't quit this? . . . It's all my fault again? Alright, just what do you want me to do, beg your forgiveness, fall down on my knees in front of you? What's the matter with you all, are you idiots, what's got into you?"

"He's even calling us idiots."

"Him."

"Us."

"He doesn't know what he's saying."

"He's like Pecker, don't you hear how he's yelling?"

Really, he was yelling, wet with sweat, infuriated with the dog who was limping and yelping.

"To hell with you," he said.

And he went into the forest almost running to escape from the cur and from them and to take another path to the village. And then they ran after him, and when he appeared again on the bank of the Danube, he was fighting against a frenzied pack of dogs with a tree branch. He came toward Miss Mia, with them following, and it seemed to me too that there wasn't anything funny about this game now and that it wasn't a game anymore when they caught hold of his pants and tore the jacket from his hands. He ran along the riverbank, but the dogs were quicker than he and they came in front of him and surrounded him and one of the more savage ones caught him by the pantleg and rolled him over in the sand.

"Get into the water," said Jeremy, and then I saw how everybody was watching him fight against the beasts. "Get into the water . . ."

"Quit joking, what the Goddamn hell's got into you?"

And again he ran down to the river's edge, but he didn't go back into the forest; here at least he had the water behind him and they couldn't corner him on all sides. He grabbed another piece of willow and got up his courage and kicked the daylights out of the ones who came at him from the marsh and whirled around in the middle of them and howled like a rabid animal with red eyes and a foaming mouth. Running at full speed he got to the place where the Saturday River flows into the Danube and he stopped short on the bank and when he looked into the clear water he took fright, either because of its depth or because he saw his eyes grown wide with fear and his face and his torn clothes and his hair standing on end and all the trembling he felt within him showing up as trembling on the shimmering surface of the river like the trembling of another being whom he didn't know. Sofronie and Jeremy and Kitchea and Bargain and Zabic came up panting, and he ran back from them and their dogs and their

idiocy, and he didn't ask for any help from them as he had
in the past, as his helpers, which is what they were to
him, as he had asked them to be earlier when the game
began, and he didn't even shout, not at them, nor at the
dogs, and he didn't utter a word, not even when he saw
her in the same place where she was before; he only
looked at her, and although when, after a moment, he did
seem to want to tell her something or to shout, his mouth
just hung open, wordless, and because he was speechless,
I couldn't make out what he was thinking or what he
wanted. The dogs didn't let up, and his fear of them and of
that insane game that was driving me out of my mind too,
made it easier for him to run, but however much he ran,
there was nowhere to escape to; going into the forest and
hiding was even more frightening to him, and maybe it
seemed impossible to him that he wouldn't be found
there, and he was too ashamed to climb a locust or the
poplar where I was; there was still in him the desire not to
be laughed at by them, so he stayed on the bank and
struck out at random and yelled and cursed, and once
again was rolled in the sand and got covered with burs,
and when he got up from among the young willows and
the locust saplings, I saw him with cow dung all over his
legs, and on his head he had a dried up shrub whose brown
leaves had fallen down, covering him, so that what remained, black and long and twisted around like some
kind of horns, were the thin, dead branches. The first dog
that ripped open the flesh on the calf of his leg, covering
him with blood, was shot on the spot by Sofronie, and the
other dogs, deafened by the shot and incited by the smell
of blood and gunpowder, jumped on the dead dog and
grabbed him in their teeth and tore him apart like an old
sock, and for a while Acatrinei escaped from their pursuit
and glared savagely at her as she leaned against a locust
tree, untroubled but still angry at him. He breathed heav-
ily, as one does after a humiliating struggle, and when the
pack of skinny bitches and floundering mastiffs jumped
up on him to knock him down, he hit them with a tree

branch as straight as a pole; and during the respites he looked at her and at them, still waiting for their joke or her vengeance to end, and since they didn't end, he couldn't understand how the wanton temper, the capriciousness, the conceit or the stupidity of a bitch of a woman could cost you your life. I had left my stilts against another poplar tree a little ways off and had come on tiptoe toward them, and I was sorry I didn't have a rifle to flatten all those dogs, and I was afraid that they might smell me with their hungry scent and would roll me over in the sand, and I climbed up into another poplar, almost to the top; I could see them all from behind. I signalled with my shirt to Acatrinei to show him I was there and that I saw him. And waving my shirt around and around in the air I called to him to come up into the tree beside me and escape from their joke, but he didn't see me. They kept shouting at him to get into the water or let himself be tied up, but he may have realized better than I what kind of trouble he was in and that there was no chance of escaping anymore from their imbecility and fear of rabies, and from her obstinacy. And then he started to yell, hoarsely, from having shouted so much; or he may have had Pecker's voice. That's how it seemed. And his wordless hoarseness (a kind of harsh groan) I heard better when he came under my poplar tree; probably he had seen my signals and the shirt. He climbed up into the poplar in agony and the dogs came and pulled him by the feet, and since his hands were all bitten and he couldn't hold himself up with them to climb, the dogs knocked him to the ground several times; but finally he managed to get away from them. Bargain laughed, pointing at him, and everybody laughed and agreed with Miss Mia when she said:

"He's really got it, he even climbs trees."

He was crying, or whimpering, sucking the bites that hurt him, and I called out his name and told him to come up higher, but he didn't hear me. They didn't come closer to the poplar, they just waited; they knew he wouldn't stay up in it all his life; up there he was much easier to tie up. They unfastened their belts and put them together so they could tie him up. The dogs were biting at each other as they looked up. Their lack of haste, not the dogs', seemed encouraging to me, and maybe he also noticed it, but it was something else that made him climb down; he saw me. His mouth dropped open like someone thunderstruck, which meant that he hadn't seen my signals with the shirt; he had climbed up in the same poplar where I was just by chance, and when he caught sight of me he got even more scared than of the dogs. And I don't know what gesture he made to me, horror-stricken and terrifying me with his terror, and he jumped into the thick of the dogs with nothing in his hands, and they moved aside and were silent for a while and didn't come any closer to him and he didn't run. Everything fell into a stillness that cloaked you couldn't tell what, and he went toward her with his hands in what was left of his pockets, dirty and ragged and silent, and then with his hands outstretched as if he were begging them to tie him up, if that was the way their game was supposed to end. They didn't tie him up, they went away, and when he started to run toward them to force them, before the dogs could reach him again, to tie him up and let him be with them, the filthy curs surrounded him with even greater ferocity, and he, seeing that once again he had missed the chance of an end to the game, wanted to get it over with any way he could; he let himself get bitten, he didn't even defend himself, in order to force them to call off their curs. But then Bargain fired at another dog. My heart beat wildly, and as I held the poplar tightly in my arms, it seemed to me that the beating entered into it, belonging to it as well, and beating as if from within its own heart. The dogs hit by small shot were even more enraged. The dead ones were pushed with tree branches into the Danube and the water took them and carried them down to the valley like gunny sacks. He came along the bank and sat down on the grass exhausted, and you could tell that either he didn't know anymore what was happening to him and was, as

they said, beaten down like Pecker, or he had lost all hope
of ever being able to escape from them alive and saw his
only salvation, if escape wasn't possible, in having his life
end as quickly as possible, and this end couldn't come
about if he struggled again for nothing, punishing himself
for nothing. They threw clumps of dirt at him, but he
didn't even flinch.

"He doesn't feel pain anymore, just like Pecker," said
Bargain.

And it was very strange for me to see how that little
freak had cured himself overnight and was now more expert in symptoms than anyone else. I didn't have a rifle
and looked all around hoping for someone to happen
along on his way to Cimpuletz, but in vain. He was getting weak and didn't care anymore about the biting and
didn't protect himself anymore against their black
mouths, and either he was like Pecker, and in that case
what they were doing was still horrifying—more exactly,
what they weren't doing—or he was letting himself be
torn apart so that, once and for all, he would be done with
what they had in mind for him, and with what the curs
had been able to do to him up to then; because fighting
only prolonged the pain for nothing and didn't gain him
anything, and maybe he couldn't bear either having them
watch him endlessly. All he did was look at them. But he
didn't look in the direction of my poplar, either because
he had forgotten me and therefore was rabid and couldn't
even keep my image in his mind in order to forget me, or
because he didn't want to lead them to the poplar with
the idea that they might find me there, and he might give
some sign that I had seen them and they might think of
me what they thought of him, or out of fear that I might
tell him to sic the dogs on me too. I don't know what
might have been in his head. But even if he was as they
said, they left him to the mercy of the curs wrongly and
unjustly, and whatever happened after that, whether he
died or not, diseased or not, they ought to pay for it with

their lives. I thought that he might die then, when he stood up once again on his feet and began to fight with the pack of dogs; he couldn't bear any longer seeing them lunge at him or hearing the gunshots that stirred them up and just stay there like a block of wood. But he was exhausted and fell to his knees, and he roused them even more by hitting them and trying to escape from them by running away. Oh God, how come the dogs went mad in our village while in other places around they went about their own business without foaming mouths, or had been taken for shots at the right time and had had their mouths looked at, why us? And then I asked myself: but what if he wasn't rabid? What if it was they, they who were trying to destroy him? And they urged on the dogs against him and were driving him to the grave, guiltless. But then, maybe they weren't guilty either. And it was even more horrifying that they would continue to live, and in the evening go into the village and unjustly put someone else in the same position. They shot their guns up into the air, filling it with the smell of burned gunpowder, and the dogs, heated up and also exhausted, pushed him up to the Danube and he started to defend himself by splashing water in their eyes, and they rushed at him and knocked him down on the bank and into the water, and in the waves you couldn't tell dog from man; they were one on top of the other like some different kind of animal made up of heads of dogs and bodies of dogs, and having the head of a man too, and the hands and feet of a man. They fired with small shot at the dogs who were afraid of the water and who wanted to come back to the shore, and forced them to stay away from the bank, and those dogs went back toward him and some of them, but only when close to him, were seized by death, carried in the bullets, and they started to float, without the breath of life, around him. The water took them and began to drown them all in a tangle and to carry them downstream, floating, but not for long. I never caught sight of him again among them and their water-logged yelping. The Danube was taking him down and what was incredible was that the sun was shining red as it was sinking into darkness, and the leaves were rustling, and there, rising, was the moon.

QUARTET ENCOUNTERS

The purpose of this paperback series is to bring together influential and outstanding works of twentieth-century European literature in translation. Each title has an introduction by a distinguished contemporary writer, describing a personal or cultural 'encounter' with the text, as well as placing it within its literary and historical perspective.

Quartet Encounters will concentrate on fiction, although the overall emphasis is upon works of enduring literary merit, whether biography, travel, history or politics. The series will also preserve a balance between new and older works, between new translations and reprints of notable existing translations. Quartet Encounters provides a much-needed forum for prose translation, and makes accessible to a wide readership some of the more unjustly neglected classics of modern European literature.

Aharon Appelfeld · *The Retreat*

Gaston Bachelard · *The Psychoanalysis of Fire*

Robert Bresson · *Notes on the Cinematographer*

Hermann Broch · *The Sleepwalkers*

E.M. Cioran · *The Temptation to Exist*

Stig Dagerman · *The Games of Night*

Grazia Deledda · *After the Divorce*